Hearts & Other Dead Things

Compiled by Cake & Quill / Angelika Rust
Edited by Catherine Lenderi
Cover Design by Charlotte Stirling

First Edition February 2016

Copyright 2016 by Cake & Quill / Angelika Rust / Catherine Lenderi / Charlotte Stirling
For further information contact:
cakeandquill@fantasymail.de

All rights reserved. Any unauthorized reprint or use of this material is prohibited. No part of this book may be reproduced or transmitted in any form or by any means, electronic or mechanical, including photocopying, recording, or by any information storage and retrieval system without express written permission from the author/publisher.
Some characters, places or events appearing in this work are based on reality; names have been changed to preserve privacy. Most are entirely fictitious, and any resemblance to real persons, living or dead, is purely coincidental. Spelling includes UK and US.

ISBN: 152394708X
ISBN-13: 978-1523947089

A word in advance

A ragged, thin Myanmar girl gripped my hand through the fence and sobbed repeatedly, 'chei-zu tin-bar-te' (thank you). I had done nothing for her except to say hello and smile. This was my emotional introduction to the dark hypocrisy that seeps into every fibre of Singapore.

The hourly abuse and modern day slavery that exist all over the city-state is almost incomprehensible. Most people ignore it. Over time the pampered living seems to blinker our eyes to the huge divide between helper and employer. Perfectly nice Western families forget their maid's birthday, or exclaim that their helper hasn't seen their children for 2 years. But don't offer to pay for them to return home.

The dehumanization of certain people, usually women, that I witnessed made me feel that I was living during Apartheid or the Holocaust and I couldn't understand why nobody else seemed bothered. Could they not see it? Seriously?

Whether making a maid walk 3 paces behind carrying all the shopping, or denying these vulnerable women any days off for months, or smacking them, or humiliating them, or rationing their food. I helped where I could. Vitamin tablets, hugs, phone calls home, extra food smuggled through the fence, and more hugs. But I had no political voice there at all and protests are illegal, so I decided to write a book. Writing is what I do. It's my talent. And I thought, just do it. Write it. Get it out there.

Tell their stories. Give them some acknowledgement. Something. Anything.

HOME is an extraordinary charity that actively helps these women to take legal action, to escape abusive employers and re-locate if necessary. They advise on contracts and employment. But most of all, they give hope when there is very little left. This is why we have chosen them as the recipient of the proceeds for this book and are proud to do so.

Charlotte Stirling, February 2016

Romantics Anonymous

Bradley Darewood / Cat Nicolaou

Magdalene took her seat quietly. She always looked forward to Tuesdays. Supposedly this was therapy, but it was a guilty pleasure, really. She loved to sit silently and listen to the tales of other people's failed relationships. They were always so juicy!

"Why is there an empty seat next to Jennifer?" Maggie asked the man next to her. She would have rather asked someone else, but Peter always seemed to find a way to sit beside her.

"It's for the new guy," Peter replied.

She thought she had sensed excitement in the air-- a new member! New stories! She couldn't wait. If she was really lucky, he'd be cute.

Her enthusiasm plummeted like a skydiver with a broken chute as her ex-boyfriend took the empty seat across the circle from her. *Jeremy. Oh. My. Fucking. God.*

Magdalene's eyes wandered around the room as he attempted to make eye contact. She should flee. She should run out of the room.

"Welcome to Romantics Anonymous!" Russ said, beginning the meeting as he sat down.

Oh god, it's too late.

Russ continued, "Now you all remember our only rule-- this is a place for sharing, not judging. Please join us in welcoming our new member, Jeremy."

Maggie clapped awkwardly along with the others,

looking at Jeremy's feet as she did.

"Now, Jeremy, the way this works is that we each get the chance to share the relationships that have scarred us. If you're not ready to share, you can take as much time as you need to warm up. There's always next week. We won't put you on the spot on your first day! Maggie, you've been here for a month now and haven't had the chance to say a word. Would you like to start us off today?"

For fuck's sake! Could this get any worse?

"I...er..."

"Come on, Maggie, don't be shy," Peter urged her.

She turned her gaze and caught him staring at her boobs as always. *My eyes are up here, you ass!* God be her witness, she was going to smack him one of these days. *Did he just flex his chest muscles?* She felt bile rising up in her mouth.

It was fun listening to Peter's stories, in the way you enjoy watching a car wreck at the movies, but there was no way she would *ever* go out with a guy like him. She had reached rock bottom lately and that would still be too low for her. *Jeremy, though...* Jeremy was a good guy. Why did she ever leave him? Maybe she wouldn't have to be in this shitty situation if she had stayed with him. And now she had to talk about all her failures in front of him. She dared a look his way. Jeremy gave her a friendly smile as if encouraging her to start. She couldn't let him know how bad things were after him. Could she?

"When you are ready, Maggie," Russ said, breaking into her musings.

"I just don't know how to begin, Russ."

"Why don't you tell us how many relationships it has been for you?" he prompted.

"That would be four," she said, attempting another look at Jeremy to check his reaction. There was none.

His face was perfectly calm.

"Would you like to tell us their names?" Russ asked again.

"Well, the last one was Patrick who insisted I call him Pat for short. The ambiguous name sorta makes sense in retrospect... and before that was Rick the Dick and before him was Tim and my first relationship was...er… let's call him John, shall we?" She saw Jeremy shifting on his seat. He knew she was talking about him.

"Would you like to start with John?" Russ asked.

Magdalene froze, her eyes locked in Jeremy's. "No. I wouldn't want to bore you."

Did Jeremy just flinch?

"I--I don't mean in a bad way--" Maggie stammered, "I just-- I'd rather talk about Tim."

"Okay. Go ahead, Maggie."

"Well, the first thing you should know is that he was incredibly handsome. Stunning eyes. You know, the ones that make you melt every time he looks at you." She smiled as one of the ladies in the circle went "Aww." Maggie continued with a dreamy tone in her voice, wishing to please her audience, "Oh and that body of his! God, that man was too hot for his own good! I think he was some sort of champion tennis player in college. Like first chair or first seat or rank or however that works for tennis. He had *amazing* abs. I just loved to roll my fingers over them. I'm telling you that man could easily be a cover model..."

Jeremy snorted.

Maggie looked at him. "But he was so much more than just a pretty face," she added quickly, not wanting to sound superficial.

Was Peter flexing again? *Christ. Your brain is smaller than your nuts.*

She rolled her eyes and continued, "and he was successful. He had a PhD in Nutrition Sciences and an

MD from Oxford. It was great dating someone who could keep up with me intellectually."

Jeremy coughed. He turned bright red as the group members turned to look at him. "Sorry, my coffee just… went down the wrong pipe."

"Keep going, Maggie," Russ said, his brow furrowed.

"Well, Tim worked full time with Doctors Without Borders. When he wasn't in West Africa fighting Ebola and starvation or whatever, he worked at the Children's Hospital downtown in the Urgent Care Unit."

"Maggie, this really doesn't sound like a traumatic relationship--" Russ began, confused.

"Russ!" From across the circle, Jennifer shushed the facilitator. She leaned forward with a captivated smile. "Go on, Maggie! He sounds divine. How did you two meet?"

"Well…" Maggie twisted her foot awkwardly. "Starbucks mixed up our coffee orders, and I, well, I asked if he'd like to go see a movie. We went on quite a few dates. Except I don't think he knew they were dates…."

Jennifer's smile turned to a look of confusion.

"You know, we'd go to the movie, and nothing would happen. I, you know, would sort of touch his hand and ask if he had a good time and... He said, 'I'd been meaning to see *Redneck Cinderella* but none of my friends like romantic comedies. I'm so glad we're friends!' Then he drove off!"

"So… wait, did you actually date this guy?" Jennifer asked.

"Of course!" Maggie said defensively. "That was just the beginning."

She felt the group's eyes on her, judging. *What happened to "this is a space for sharing," you assholes?*

"Alright, fine. The first three months of the relationship were like that. The actual relationship was two weeks long."

"Did you ever… tell him he was... in a relationship with you?" Russ asked, puzzled.

Maggie glanced at Jeremy, struggling to keep the color from rising in her cheeks. This was *not* going as she planned. "Of course! It just… took three months. Finally, what happened was we were having lunch and the waitress, she was mooning all over him. I mean like she may as well have taken her breasts out in the middle of the restaurant the way she kept leaning over and shoving them in his face. But he totally didn't even notice."

"So you finally got the courage to ask him out?" Jennifer said, smiling again.

"Well… uh, not exactly. The waitress came with the bill. She sort of slid it under his plate, giving him doe eyes the whole time. But he had to use the restroom so he got up without checking it. The whole thing was suspicious, so as soon as he left, I pulled the check out and that *slut* had drawn hearts all over it! 'You have beautiful eyes,' it said. And she left her phone number!"

"What did you do?" Jennifer asked in shock.

"Well, I was furious of course. That was the last straw. I took the pen and scrawled over her number until it was completely black. I even tore through the paper. That's when Tim got back from the restroom. He asked 'Is everything okay?' and I just froze. I was like, 'Um, yeah,' and he took the bill from me and just stared at it for a while. Finally, he said: 'You… think I have beautiful eyes?' and I said yes, and from that moment we were dating."

"For two weeks," Jeremy interjected, a hint of sarcasm in his voice.

"You don't understand what it was like to be with him," Maggie replied hotly. Her eyes challenged him.

"No, but I'm sure you'll enlighten us," Jeremy

replied.

"Fine. For your information," she started, looking straight at him, "Tim was awesome in bed. Very passionate and quite adventurous, if you know what I mean. During his travels around the world he had picked up quite some tricks."

She saw Jeremy lower his gaze. She smiled in satisfaction. She had won this round. Jeremy had been her first, and she always remembered how sweet it was to be with him. But... he never wanted to try anything new. With Tim she had felt freer, more like herself, because she could experiment.

"I still don't see what was wrong with this guy," Jennifer interrupted her.

"Well, the man's only free time was from midnight until about 6am. The first two days we were dating, I would drive all the way to his apartment and we would have sex, and then I wanted to cuddle and spend some time with him, but he would either pass out cold or get up and go because there was always some kind of a crisis somewhere in his world."

Peter humphed. "You do know that a man has to work, don't you, sugar?"

"Well, I work too, you know," she answered back, barely restraining a deluge of cusswords that always crossed her mind when that Neanderthal spoke. "But what's the point in trying to form a relationship if you can't spend time with your partner?"

"So what happened?" Jennifer asked again.

"The third day was my birthday. We'd spoken about it like a week ago. He asked what sign I was and I said I was born on the very first day of Aquarius, so he should have figured out that my birthday was Wednesday."

"You've got to be kidding, darling," Peter said, his arms folded.

"I'm not your darling, and no, I'm not kidding--" She

bit her tongue. She didn't want to get kicked out of the group for verbally assaulting Peter. "Well, I thought he might be too busy and it may have slipped his mind so I decided to take matters into my own hands."

"Go on!" Jennifer said, enraptured.

"I bought myself this incredibly sexy lingerie, like the kind you need a Brazilian wax to wear--" *Was Peter grabbing his crotch?* Maggie paused to eye him in disgust before continuing. "I bought a box of chocolates in a silver heart-shaped box with a 'happy birthday' note on top of it. *And* I baked a cake! His favorite kind: chocolate with cream cheese frosting."

Jeremy twisted. "You never baked--" his voice caught in his throat, "I mean, did you… ever bake your other boyfriends a cake?"

Maggie looked at him flatly, pointedly ignoring his question before moving on. "I put the cake in the refrigerator and set the table… and he was nowhere to be found!" She paused for a moment. "Of course, I called him," she replied to the unspoken question in Jennifer's eyes. "But there was no answer."

Jennifer tsked.

"I tried not to be furious. He must be working late, right? So I decided to lie on his bed, waiting for him in my sexy lingerie, box of chocolates in hand."

Peter gripped his crotch again. Maggie wanted to kick him.

"When I woke up… the box of chocolates was gone! On the back he'd scrawled a note: 'Thanks for the grub-- it'll make a great lunch. And it's not even my birthday!' I punched the pillow and screamed."

Peter snickered. Maggie really was going to punch him.

"And the cake?" Jeremy asked.

He's really stuck on that cake. "He missed it, thank God. I took it home with me. As soon as I got there, I called him up and demanded to know where he was the night before. He didn't sound sorry at all-- he was giddy and excited! There was a midnight showing of a documentary he'd been wanting to see about saving homeless children in Vietnam or some horseshit and he and his colleagues had gone out!"

Maggie took a deep breath, trying to calm herself. "I was shocked. I had done all these preparations and he didn't even bother to call and tell me. I mean he could have called and invited me to come, at which point I could have told him he had to come home. I mean, that's how relationships work, right? I was ready to give him the fight of his life. I mean how could he be so insensitive!? But then I thought that since we had only started dating, I should give him some slack. Maybe this was just all new to him. So I thought I give him another chance."

"How did that work for you then?" Russ asked this time.

"It didn't, actually. The next day, I came over and made him dinner. I brought the cake and lingerie again, hoping everything would work out this time. So I left him waiting at the table and went in the kitchen to get the dessert. I got undressed, save that hot lingerie I had bought just for him, grabbed the cake and the chocolate syrup and swayed back into the dining room. His eyes dilated when he saw me and I thought that I had caught his attention this time and we were going to have a night of hot sex."

"Finally!" Jennifer said.

Maggie shook her head. "The fool I was! He got up, snatched the cake and the syrup from my hand and plopped himself in front of the TV to watch a tennis match. I stood there speechless staring at him. 'Tim, aren't we... going to do anything tonight?' I asked him after a long moment. 'Sure, we are,' he replied. 'Tonight it's the Wimbledon finals! Have a seat. God this cake is good!' Needless to say, I fell asleep after ten minutes of looking at a ball going back and forth. He finished the whole cake and I still don't think he figured out it was my birthday."

"So let me get this straight. He had you half naked and watched TV?" Peter sneered.

Maggie ignored his remark.

"He must be gay," Peter said.

She snapped this time. "He was not!"

"All I can tell you is that a *real man* would never leave such a beautiful creature unattended." Peter licked his lips.

Maggie shuddered. "I am *not* a creature."

"And your ex-boyfriend wasn't a real man."

"I'll tell you how much of a real man he was. On those nights he *was* in the mood, his hard--"

Jeremy cleared his throat, shifting uncomfortably.

Maggie blushed, realizing she may have crossed a line.

"Peter, if you're done reminding us you're a man, will you shut the fuck up and let her finish her story?" Jennifer interfered. "Go on, Maggie. I guess you left him after that."

"Uh, no...I thought that he might have been tired and not in the mood for sex, so I let it go. The next two days, he was off work so we went out and had lots of fun, and I said to myself that the problems were gone and we would be fine; but then he went missing again for a couple of days and wouldn't answer any of my calls. So it was Friday, I think, when I decided to go find him at the hospital. I got into my car and took the highway, but halfway I got a flat tire. Luckily, I managed to stop the car in time and was safe but a little shaken, to tell you the truth. I called him and this time he picked up immediately. 'Oh, thank God you answered,' I said and asked where he had been the last couple of days. 'Working,' he replied. 'Are you at the hospital now?' I asked then. 'No,' he just said. 'Ok, so where are you?' I asked again, really trying to keep my calm. 'Out.' His one-word replies were starting to get on my nerves. 'With?' I wondered. 'Friends,' he replied. 'Look, Tim, I think we should talk and right now I have a problem and I need your help.' 'What's up?' he asked. 'Well, I missed you and I wanted to see you so I got into my car but--' 'Oh, it's my turn at the pool table. Talk later.' He hung up on me. Just like that!"

"What a jerk!" Jennifer exclaimed, trying not to laugh.

"It's not funny!" Maggie replied defensively. "The guy can help starving children in Africa or wherever but he can't be bothered to help me with a flat tire?"

"The starving children are probably clearer about what they want," Jeremy said flatly.

Maggie shot barbs at him with her eyes, then continued with her story. "I called him the next day to break up with him. 'We need to talk,' I said. 'What's up, babe? I'm about to go into surgery' was all he had to say. I told him I thought things weren't working out-- I don't think he understood because he said: 'Hey gotta go!' I stopped calling him and he didn't call back until a month later, to see if I wanted to have sex."

"He didn't notice you broke up with him for a whole month?" Jennifer said in disbelief.

"Nope."

"Did you…"

"God no! I told him where he could stick it." Maggie took a sip of coffee. It was getting cold.

"How do you feel, Maggie? I know sharing can be hard," Russ said.

"It's okay. It's cathartic really."

"Let's take a break for a couple of seconds."

Maggie was first to stand, walking to the table for a

refill. *Oh god. Jeremy's right behind me.* She felt the temperature rising in her face. She wasn't sure if it was anger or embarrassment.

"Hey--" Jeremy began, then paused, a concerned look on his face. "You're really red."

"I have a sunburn."

"I don't think--"

"Look, are you following me? I've had a stalker and--"

"Mags, I swear I never expected to see you here."

He always called her Mags when they were together. "That makes two of us."

"I quite enjoyed your story," he said with a gentle smile.

Was he *laughing* at her? "Really? Well, wait till I get to 'John'. Let's see if you find that one amusing then," she snapped.

Jeremy nearly dropped his coffee as she brushed past him to her seat.

"Shall I continue with the rest of them, Russ," she asked, "or would it be better if someone else spoke, like Jeremy there, for example?"

Jeremy quickly took his seat, a look of alarm on his face.

"You can go on," Russ said.

"Well, after Tim I needed a man who could appreciate me," she began. "I met Rick three months later. One day my friend Mary asked me to join a yoga class with her. I had heard that yoga is great exercise. So, we went for our first session. It was fun, though a bit harder than I expected. The instructor came to talk to us after class. He had so much to say about the philosophy of yoga.

Rick was an amazing speaker. So confident and eloquent. I was fascinated. I could listen to him talk for hours about Eastern culture and religion. When he wasn't all sweaty in his yoga pants, he had that professor look, you know, glasses and well-ironed shirts. But mixed with such a sexy Australian accent. He liked to say 'mate' a lot. You wouldn't call him pretty exactly, but he had that... special something… that women find very attractive."

"Special something?" Jeremy asked in confusion.

"Well, yoga pants leave little to the imagination. And after our first date, I confirmed he was very *qualified*."

"Hence, the nickname, right?" said Jennifer, smiling.

Maggie returned her smile. "Well, he did have a big package which he absolutely adored, but that's not the only reason I called him a dick."

"Ok, define big," Peter chimed in, spreading his knees apart.

"You don't have to go into that kind of detail, Maggie," Russ said, casting a disapproving glance at Peter.

"Oh, no, do tell," Jennifer pleaded. "I want to hear this."

"You really don't have to..." Jeremy bit his lip uncomfortably.

"Well, if you must know, he was enormous. I never asked for exact measurements but it was almost… *inhuman*," she replied, looking at Jeremy.

"That good, huh?" Jennifer asked.

"I'll tell you one thing only. At first, I was scared when I saw it, but when he did that slow thrust of his, I saw stars every single time. And he was a sex machine. He never got tired of sex with me. Best orgasms I had ever had."

"Why on earth did you ever let that man go, then?" Jennifer wondered.

"Well, he wasn't exactly right for me."

"What did he do? Did he cheat on you?"

"Uh, no. It wasn't that, but he did things I didn't like.

First of all, he masturbated a lot."

"Oh come on. All guys do that! We just relieve tension," Peter interrupted again.

"I know but… you don't understand. It was like this. We had all that sex and then I would catch him sitting in front of the TV playing with himself, and he'd be watching… *sports*. Who masturbates to American football? Whenever I skyped him, I could see his hand move up and down while we were talking. On the phone sometimes he'd make these weird grunts. At first, I thought it was kinda sexy. You know, even just talking on the phone, he found me so hot he couldn't resist temptation. Everything was great in the beginning, but then it started getting a bit… I don't know...creepy maybe…"

"Creepy?" Russ asked.

"He seemed so sweet. Always texting me to ask where I was. Like he was really involved in my day."

"That's not very creepy."

"Any day I broke my routine-- to go to the grocery store, or take a walk, I would get a text message, in all caps: 'WHERE ARE YOU?' If I replied with 'at home', I'd get a text: 'NO YOU'RE NOT.' It was a little disconcerting."

"It's good to pay attention to those sort of gut feelings," Russ said, troubled.

"It took me a few weeks to figure it out. I found out later from my neighbor that he waited outside my house every day to make sure I came home from work, sometimes he'd even ask her where I was."

"That's a bad sign." Russ crossed his arms.

"Once I found that out, every time he'd text 'Where are you?' it didn't feel sweet. It felt creepy."

"I hope you broke up with him after that."

"I mean, yes, he was creepy, but I also felt… needed. He was so insatiable *with* me. I couldn't imagine what he would have done *without* me. And he would say such sweet things."

"What sort of sweet things?" Russ asked skeptically.

"Well, when we were deep in the throes of passion, and I mean *deep*--"

"Really?" Jeremy asked, clumsily crossing his legs in an attempt to look indifferent.

Maggie continued, casting an accusing glance at Jeremy, "He said... 'You're mine.'"

"That was... sweet?" Russ was baffled.

"Of course it was! After Tim's utter negligence, it felt great to be the center of his universe."

"Women love to be possessed," Peter agreed with a smug smirk.

Maggie threw up a little bit in her mouth. She was getting back-up from *Peter*. "I-- I wouldn't go that far--"

"It's true!" Peter protested.

"Peter, shhhhh." Jennifer put her finger to her lips. "That's enough of men talking for the moment." She turned to Maggie, "Go on, dear."

"Well, it was sweet when he said it in bed. He would spoon me and put his hand over my heart and just whisper 'You're mine' into my hair. It made me feel so loved, but then he'd... I don't know, say it out of bed. At one point I had coffee with a friend from high school. He was going to Morocco and since I've been there on holiday, he wanted to ask me about good spots to visit. I didn't tell Rick of course-- he would have lost his shit, but he must have found out by reading my email."

"How did he read your email?" Jeremy sat forward, alarmed.

"Well, I gave him my password. He asked and I didn't really want to tell him no…"

Jeremy smacked his forehead in frustration.

"That sounded like passing judgement," Maggie accused icily.

"I didn't say anything!" Jeremy protested.

"She's right," Russ interjected. "Jeremy, you're new. Please try to be more careful."

Jeremy gripped the sides of his seat so hard his hands turned white.

"Well, after that meeting, my friend never returned my calls. I didn't figure out why for months. Apparently, Rick had followed us to the cafe, then followed him home. He told my friend that now he knew where he lived, and that he'd cut him if he ever spoke to me again because I could only be his."

"He sounds terrible," Jennifer whispered.

"Yeah, he'd go through my old Facebook pictures, demanding to know who this person was or that person was. He was so rude he'd drive my friends away. He'd go through my phone regularly to see who was texting me. I finally demanded to go through his and it was… almost like he liked it. He liked that I was jealous and controlling enough to want to see his phone. That's when I saw the pictures."

"The pictures?" Jennifer asked.

"Well, first there were plenty of pictures of his dick. Seriously, what kind of freak takes so many pictures of his own genitals?"

Peter coughed. Jeremy and Russ repositioned themselves awkwardly on their chairs, looking at their feet.

Maggie continued, "But it was the pictures between his dick pics that I found disturbing. Pictures of me getting out of the car to go to work, shopping, sleeping. Like millions of pictures. In a lot of them I looked just awful. I mean, who takes your picture when you're not ready?"

Jennifer opened her mouth to speak but closed it, confused.

"So I dumped him of course."

"You… dumped him because you didn't like the way you looked in the pictures he took, or you dumped him because he was stalking you?" Jeremy asked for clarification.

"Well, I guess when you put it that way… maybe both."

"Both?"

"Look, if you bothered trying to look good, maybe you'd understand. Anyway, Rick didn't take the breakup well."

"What happened?" Jeremy wondered.

"He kept calling me all day long; he would come and knock on my door, crying and begging to see me. He promised he was going to change but then I would say something to him and see his obsession emerge again. So I told him not to come back again or else I would call the police."

"He didn't stay away for long, right?" Russ remarked.

"No, but that's how I met Patrick, my latest ex-boyfriend. You see, about a month later, I was returning from work and noticed Rick's car in the distance, waiting outside my home. At that moment, my neighbor was coming out of his house, so I grabbed his arm and asked for his help. He told me to go home and he would have a word with Rick. My neighbor Patrick was a strong man, Martial Arts and all, I was sure Rick wouldn't stand a chance against him if they got into a fight."

"Did he kick his ass?" Peter asked with a smug grin on his face.

"Not exactly," Maggie said wryly.

"Well, what happened?"

"I didn't see, but Patrick knocked on my door shortly thereafter. He assured me that Rick was long gone, and wasn't coming back any time soon, but he had a concerned look on his face. Like he was troubled by something."

"So he didn't kick his ass?" Peter asked, confounded.

"No, Peter, he didn't." *Seriously, Peter's brain must be located in his penis.* "I invited Patrick in for some tea-- it was the least I could do-- and I asked him what happened. He told me Rick claimed that *I* was obsessed with *him.*"

"Wow! What an asshole!" Jennifer exclaimed.

"I know, right? Why would *his* car be outside *my* house if that were the case? I assured him that that was absurd and Patrick's response was: 'But have you seen that guy's dick?'"

"Wait--what?" Jeremy said in confusion.

"I think he was implying that a dick like that might make any girl obsessed."

"No, I mean-- how in the hell did he see Rick's dick?" Jeremy's brow was furrowed.

"I asked the same question. He was sort of uncomfortable for a moment, then he told me that the creep had a photo of mine on the steering wheel and was stroking his dick!"

A disturbed groan spread throughout the room.

Maggie continued, "What's worse was, he didn't even bother to cover himself when he saw Pat!"

"Wow," Peter said, "his dick must have been really big."

"Christ, Peter. His dick wasn't near as big as his ego. Patrick was still uncomfortable. He reached into his pocket and pulled out *a wedding ring.* He put it back on, but I had to ask why he took it off."

"Please tell me you didn't date a married man," Jennifer admonished.

"His wife was a complete bitch," Maggie replied. "The opposite of Patrick. He was so sweet. He was so embarrassed when he told me that he'd hidden it before he walked to Rick's car. He told Rick that he was my boyfriend! He apologized immediately for lying without my permission. He was so well-mannered and adorable."

Jeremy raised an eyebrow.

Maggie went on, "I was quite shaken-up after Patrick told me what had happened. I was sure that Rick would never leave me alone. I started crying involuntarily and Patrick was so tender and comforting and I hate to admit it but I didn't even realize how we ended up in bed that day. Sex was great with him. Patrick was older than me, at forty-five, and he knew exactly how to worship a woman's body. We connected on a different level that day, it wasn't just physical. We started dating immediately after that and it felt so easy and comfortable to be around him."

"But he was *married,* honey," Jennifer scolded.

"I don't know why but it didn't matter. Usually, I would never go with a married man, but there was something about Patrick I couldn't resist. He could see into my female psyche. He knew all my needs without me having to say anything out loud and he would make sure they were fulfilled. It was like he knew what a woman *thinks.* I fell for him so quickly that I didn't care if I had to share him with his wife. Though, to be honest, I don't think he really loved her anyway. His marriage seemed to be more of a convention. He told me that she had helped him expand his business when they first were married and that she lorded it over his head all the time. Their relationship was more like a business partnership with a demanding partner that contributes nothing. But with me... he treated me like a queen and he bought me all these gifts and took me with him on business trips in Europe. For almost a year, I was having the time of my life."

"On second thought, that doesn't sound half bad. I'm starting to wish I had met him first," Jennifer cooed.

"I don't think you know what you are wishing for,"

Maggie replied.

Jennifer raised another eyebrow.

"Don't get me wrong. He was incredible. The man was a cosmetic genius. His night and morning regimen involved creams I've never heard of, used by models in Milan. I'm still using it, actually. Then there were the shopping trips to Paris. Patrick had *excellent* taste in clothes and he always gave the best advice on what to buy. Compared to Pat, my girlfriends were utterly tasteless. And after-- in our five-star hotel-- the way he'd kiss me and lick my breasts! He was so good at it. He could give me an orgasm just from the way his tongue circled my--"

"Ahem," Jeremy interrupted, clearing his throat.

"I felt so incredibly comfortable with him in bed that I well… expanded my horizons."

"How, exactly?" Peter said, leaning forward.

"Well, there was the whole butt thing."

Jeremy sat up straight, "You… in your…"

"No! God! *His* butt."

Jeremy's face contorted in confusion. "His…"

"I really liked to grab his ass during sex. It was unusually big for a guy's ass. First, he asked me to slap it and then…. I had heard that some guys, straight guys I mean, like it because of all the nerves that are there and it makes them cum harder. As he did too. We had great sex the first time I did that to him. He became so enthusiastic."

"Wait, you put your finger in his--" Jeremy began, trying to wrap his mind around it.

"I've heard… some… guys like that sort of thing…" Peter shifted in his seat. There was a hint of defensiveness in his voice.

"Look, the sex was great. The shopping was great. It was like having a best friend and a fantastic lover all at once. There was just one problem."

"He was married," Jennifer finished, nodding.

"He didn't even love her!" Maggie said defensively. "But sometimes I would get jealous. I mean why does she get to be his wife? I was picking out perfume in Milan one time and he wasn't even paying attention to the samples, he was texting *her.* So I confronted him."

"About texting his wife?" Jeremy asked, confused.

"He said they weren't even having sex anymore. So I just asked why he texts her so much. And he said: 'You mean, like you text Rick?' I was stunned. I hadn't seen Rick in months. He went on, 'He told me you've been harassing him and won't leave him alone.'"

"Rick *told* him?" Jennifer said, aghast.

"Exactly! When the hell did he see Rick? He suddenly got embarrassed. He stammered 'Well-- I mean-- he gave me his number.' I asked when he got Rick's number. And he puffed his chest out and said, 'That day I told him to fuck off and leave you alone.'"

"So he went to beat up Rick, saw his dick and took his number?" Peter said with a smile.

"Pretty much," Maggie said grimly.

"If a real man--" Peter started.

"Shut the fuck up, Peter."

Russ opened his mouth to speak but after a glower from Maggie, he stopped.

"A month later," Maggie folded her arms together angrily, "I saw a car parked across the street from my apartment. Rick's car!"

"I hope you called the police," Russ said, a look of concern on his face.

"He had the gall to stalk me, spread lies about me, interfere with my relationship with Pat-- I was furious. I stormed across the street to his car to tell him off once and for all. I banged on his car window. He wasn't even in there. Then I heard some rustling in the bushes nearby so I shrieked his name: 'Rick, you fucking dick! I know you're out there!'"

Jeremey winced and rubbed his ear.

Had she actually shrieked just now? She didn't care, she was furious. "I hear his sleazy Aussie voice say, 'See, mate! I told you how crazy bitches get. She just can't let go of me' and he stands up from behind the bushes, completely naked. I had to squeeze my fists as hard as I could to keep from slapping him. 'Who are you talking to? I don't even care. I'm calling the police this time!' I pulled out my phone. 'I'm going to get a restraining order and you're going to *jail.*'"

"Good for you," Russ said, clapping his hands together.

"Well, I didn't call."

"You what?"

"He wasn't there to see me."

"How did you know he wasn't there to see you?"

"He looked down and said, 'You're gonna have to come out.' There was a muffled 'no', but then he grinned at me and said, 'Babe, I'm not here to see you. I'm here to see Pat.'"

"You've got to be kidding," Jennifer said.

"So there I was, with Rick and Pat naked in the bushes. All this time I thought he'd been texting his wife, he had been texting Rick! I didn't know what to say. I just stared at Pat, utterly bewildered. Until I said, 'Why?' His answer: 'Have you *seen* his dick?'"

Maggie took a deep breath and crossed her legs.

Russ mirrored her. "Are you… is that..."

Maggie nodded. "And so it ended with Rick's dick. I'll never date again."

"Well, that was quite the story!" Russ said, sitting back. "I suppose we have time for one more person to share today if any of you--"

"I'll go."

Everyone turned to look at Jeremy.

"You really don't have to go on your first day--" Russ began.

"I think it's okay," Maggie interjected. "It's only been one day but it's like we've known him for… years."
Your turn, smart ass.

Jeremy accepted her challenge levelly. "I'd love to share, Russ. If that's okay with you."

"Of course, go ahead."

"Well, my situation is a little different than all of yours."

Maggie eyed him skeptically.

Jeremy continued, "I haven't gone from one bad relationship to another. I try, I really do. Not to have a bad relationship, I mean. To have any relationship. I just… I just can't."

"What do you mean?" Jennifer asked, putting her hand on his leg sympathetically.

Maggie bristled. She didn't like her touching him like that.

"You must have had at least one relationship," Russ said.

"I did. Only one."

Oh god. Maggie sunk deep into her chair. *He's going to talk about… me.*

"Well, it must have been horrible if you haven't dated since!" Jennifer cooed.

Maggie accidentally choked on some of her coffee.
Jennifer's hand was still on his thigh.

"That's just it…"
Here it comes.
"It wasn't."
Wait--what?
"It was the best relationship I've ever had."

"It was the *only* relationship you've ever had, Jeremy," Russ said.

"I mean, it's the best relationship, the only

relationship... I'd ever *want* to have."

Maggie's heart skipped a beat.

"I just keep going over it again and again, trying to figure out what I did wrong. What I did to lose her--"

Maggie wanted to disappear. Die and disappear. A thousand times. If only she could sink into the floor....

"What was she like?" Jennifer asked, her voice dripping with sympathy.

"Did she have big tits?" Peter added.

"Christ, Peter," Maggie snapped. Cautiously she added, "Did she?"

Jeremy smiled. "They were perfect. Everything about her was perfect. Even the imperfect things. The way she constantly says the wrong thing, or puts her foot in her mouth. The cute little way she snores at night--"

"Could you... go back to the perfect things?" Maggie interrupted.

"Yes, I could tell you her eyes were beautiful." He looked at Peter. "And her tits." He looked back at Maggie. "But it was the... intangible things. She had sort of a strength to her. Her personality was light and joyful, like sunlight. She was fun and passionate and beautiful all at once like a force of nature. Who wouldn't love someone like that?"

Maggie realized she'd been holding her breath, and let out a deep sigh.

Jeremy looked down. "I just don't know what went wrong."

"There must have been something," Jennifer prompted.

Get your hand off his leg, you cow.

"She just got distant. Like maybe she was... I don't know... bored."

Well... what do you do with a guy who already wants you? Who's already... perfect. "Oh god," Maggie whispered to herself, clutching her neck. *Perfect.*

"Did you want to say something, Maggie?" Russ asked.

"No-- I-- was-- just clearing my throat."

Russ nodded. "So, Jeremy, if you saw her again today, after all that pain she put you through, would you even want to be with her again?"

"I'd take her back, Russ. In a heartbeat."

It seemed to take ages for the meeting to end. Maggie wished she had been kinder to Jeremy in their brief exchange while refilling coffee.

At long last, Russ called the meeting to a close.

Jeremy stood across the room, chatting with Jennifer. Maggie could wait. She'd be casual about it. Jennifer twirled her hair while she spoke to him. Was she… flirting? *Oh my god, she just looked at Jeremy's package!*

Suddenly, Peter blocked her view.

"You're always so quick to get out of here." His eyes narrowed. "I'm glad you decided to linger so you could talk to me."

"Peter, I'm not--"

"Sh-- you don't need to admit it. It can be our unspoken secret." He pulled out his phone.

"I'm not giving you my phone number."

"I was just checking messages. These meetings only last an hour, but what can I say I'm a popular guy." He put the phone back in his pocket and pulled out a piece of paper and handed it to her. "If you decide you… need a real man to talk to."

Maggie looked down at the paper with Peter's number scrawled on it. "Do you keep a bunch of these already written in your pocket?" she asked, repulsed.

"Of course. Not."

"Excuse me."

Maggie pushed past Peter. At this point she didn't care about looking casual.

Jennifer had her arm in his. The woman moved fast. "You can't let one woman define you, Jeremy. You really *do* need to play the field." Jennifer's voice was sultry.

That slut! Maggie slid her arm into Jennifer's, doing her best to turn an intimate moment into a scene from the Wizard of Oz. "It's really not worth it." Maggie interjected icily, "Jennifer's played the field several times over, and still hasn't found a man that would stick."

Jennifer stiffened. "You're right, I'm an experienced woman with my fair share of rejections. But I can say I've never gone so far as to turn a man gay. I'm impressed, Maggie."

Color rose in Maggie's cheeks. The gloves were off. She opened her mouth to reply when Jeremy stopped her.

"Maggie, I did love your stories. Would you mind, maybe... taking a walk with me?"

Sunset gently touched the trees as they strolled outside. Birds were chirping love songs. It didn't take them long to find their way back to his apartment.

"I didn't realize you lived so close," she said and followed him up the stairs.

So many memories flooded her mind the moment she stepped in his apartment. How caring and tender Jeremy had always been with her. *Why did I ever let him go?*

"Do you want some tea?"

"No." She kissed him.

Looking at him now, as he was taking his clothes off slowly putting on a striptease just for her, she couldn't help thinking how different he looked. So much more confident and his body was more muscular...

She caught the shirt he playfully threw at her and beamed. He had changed. He had never danced like that for her before. Maybe listening to her stories made him understand what she wanted from a man. Variety...adventure…

Jeremy stood naked before her, already at full-mast, only by seeing her on his bed. Maggie beckoned him closer with her finger. Never dropping his eye-contact, he climbed onto the bed and touched her breasts over her bra.

"Well, since you like being licked," he said and freed one nipple.

Maggie's breath caught when his tongue touched her skin. *Finally, he is going to give me what I need.* She got hold of his hair, and waited to feel the rush she always felt with Patrick. And waited… and waited…

What the hell he is doing? She raised her head a bit and looked at him. Her breast was covered in so much saliva it made her queasy.

"Um, Jeremy, I think that's enough...um, maybe try something else now," she told him in as sweet a tone as she could muster. She didn't want to upset him since he was actually trying this time.

"Did I do alright?" he asked anxiously.

"Yeah, yeah, great… I would just like something else today," she replied.

"Maybe lick you somewhere else?" he asked with a sly smile.

"Er...okay."

Jeremy removed her panties and spread her legs open revealing a ring. "When did you do that?" he asked. "You didn't have it when we were together."

"Yeah, Patrick insisted and then I kinda neglected to go remove it."

"Uh, how do I go about it now then?" he asked, rubbing his chin. "Won't I hurt you or something?"

Maggie raised a brow. *Are you for real?* "No??"

"But what if my tongue gets stuck there? Won't that hurt you or worse, me?"

"Uh, Jeremy, are you going to do it or are we going to keep talking about it?" She was starting to lose patience and all her mood for sex now.

"I just don't know how to now… It looks so odd with that thingy there. Why did you have to go do that? I don't like it."

"Well, I certainly didn't do that for you…" Her irritation was evident in her voice.

"I know but still, you were never into kinky things," he said accusingly.

"And how would you know, Jeremy? You never asked me about my fantasies or what I would like to try, you just…" she trailed off, seeing him lowering his gaze. She regretted her tone now. She had decided to give him a second chance after all by coming here, so she said, "Look, I'm sorry, let's just make love as we used to, ok?"

Jeremy grinned and started kissing her, all the while positioning himself between her thighs. "Ok, baby, here I come then…" he said, after a long passionate kiss.

"Jeremy, are you in?" she asked after a moment.

"Of course, I am in. What…"

Oh, my God! After Rick, he feels so small. "Hehe, I was just joking," she smiled to him awkwardly. "You feel so good, big guy!"

Jeremy proudly continued his strokes until he felt he was reaching his climax about ten minutes later. She'd never been so glad that a man could finish so quickly. "Yes, yes," Maggie shouted when he looked at her waiting for confirmation that she was there as well.

She hadn't felt a thing the whole time.

"This is like a dream come true. I never thought I'd see you again. It's like I haven't felt whole since you left me. I went to that group for some sort of help moving on and… I just can't believe you're here."

Oh god. I feel ill.

Jeremy lay next to her with a satisfied smile on his face. "That was so intense, baby. You're a fire!"

"Yes, thanks!" she said and started getting off bed.

"Where are you going? Aren't you going to spend the night here?"

"Um, I'd love to but I have to work in the morning and I…"

"Well, call me tomorrow then. Or I'll see you on the next meeting."

"Yeah, sure," she said, zipping her dress. "Don't get up. I know the way."

Romantics Anonymous never saw Maggie again.

J Cassidy

I know a diamond
glittering
shattered into pieces.
Put herself back.
Now she's got cracks
and glitters even more.
Diamonds don't break.

Cake & Quill

El Hambre De Las Calaveras (The Hungry Skulls)

Charlotte Stirling

Simon de Smet of Antwerp, Belgium, married Rosa Maria Martinez of Guanajuato, Mexico, on October 31st, 2015. It was a glorious Singapore day and the (much) younger bride had chosen a dress of ivory silk that clung and flowed with breathtaking ease down her supple body. Simon, fat and ecstatic, bounced around his reception, drinking far too much of the fine burgundy wine, chosen especially by the Sommelier from the Raffles Hotel for the wedding.

The bridegroom's friends, expansive, wealthy expats and a coterie of other middle-aged mishaps, leered at the luscious Rosa, who unusually had no family attending her wedding, just a few beautiful but silent women as attendants.

She rose above it all with a stoicism that she had learnt in the House of Witches, one of the most haunted places in Mexico and now the largest brothel in the landlocked city of Léon. Rosa didn't care much for her Belgian husband and she countered his brutish advances with daydreams of cheap wood coffins and garrotes.

Simon was the CEO of one of the largest Dutch/Brazilian companies in Mexico, giving him an estimated annual bonus of two million USD. The company was run by 'wetbacks in suits', the fat man was fond of saying, and that 'Singapore suited him with its preference for multimillionaires who could sail close to the wind and never be reprimanded'.

The Belgian hated Mexicans with a passion, calling them 'monkeys', 'spics' and 'peasants', so it could be thought odd that he had chosen a beautiful Latina as his bride.

In truth, there was nothing strange about it; just the usual fat, wealthy man who could have his pick of woman and chose his bride from one of the poorest countries in the world to dominate and punch with a regularity that would not be out of place in the Politician Bar, Glasgow.

Rosa's payoff would be a hefty pre-nuptial payment in the case of divorce and a life of luxury during the marriage.

If you looked very closely you might catch the fading violet flare of a bruise on the bride's jawline, but it was difficult because of the expert bridal makeup and Simon's promise to his mother, a cruel and harsh woman, that he wouldn't punch his betrothed for a full month before their nuptials. He had come close to fulfilling this promise.

Rosa's outward serenity and placid demeanor harboured a rage so intense that it lit up her guts like fire on an oil slick. Unable to use this anger against Simon in particular, but all men in general, Rosa used every resource available to her to abuse her Pilipino housekeeper, Dumadora.

Daily, ritual humiliations were exacted. Cutting the lawn with nail scissors, eating out of a dog bowl, withholding wages and burning the maid's passport.

Every sin, every dark spot, every lash and punch that had ever been visited on Rosa, she now flung at her maid, until Dumadora was tarred and feathered with abuse.

But Dumadora was a devout, selfless woman with a soul so clean, so straight and true, that she bore these monstrous acts with the dignity and sacrifice of St.

Gianna. Every Sunday, she crept out of the house and attended early Mass where she prayed for the health of her children left behind in Leyte in the care of their Grandmother.

Her tiny, windowless room dwarfed by the huge house of stone and marble wasn't much at all, with only a mat to sleep on, the cheapest of soaps and a blue cotton rag to wash with. But in a crack, half way up the grey painted wall that housed the door, Dumadora kept her most precious thing. A creased picture of her children, taken years before but still offering comfort in the dark hours. If she held it to her chest, her heart would beat more slowly, her body relaxing in the warmth of a mother's love.

And, if she held the photograph up to her nose and inhaled, she could smell her children as newborns, sweet and milky. This single thing gave her comfort like a soft blanket for a cherished child or tall whiskey on a sullen, wind-whipped night in the Rio Grande.

Later that night the de Smets returned to the hollow, cold mansion off the Tanglin Road lapped by moonlight and the choking humidity of Singapore. The only houses close by were the towering 'black and whites' colonials of the bygone days and the inscrutable embassy buildings, grey and uncompromising like Eastern Bloc tenements.

The De Smets had jointly rejected the idea of a honeymoon; faced with an extended time under the auspices of 'love' was just too much for them.

Once the driver had dropped the couple at the towering stone door, Simon didn't even wait for the car to turn the corner, taking Rosa roughly under a crimson frangipani tree, grunting and sweating with hate and drink. When he was finished, he pushed Rosa casually onto the brittle emerald grass, her ivory dress rucked up to her hips, rich, green smudges ruining the delicate fabric.

The bride of ten hours was so full of white-hot anger; so molten with humiliation that she stumbled when she got to her feet. She wanted to hurt something and she found her way to Dumadora's room where a faint glow from underneath the door indicated that her maid was still awake, not that her sleeping would have made any difference.

Rosa kicked the door and stood barefoot, expensive high heels in hand waiting for the maid to start violently and then kneel quickly, head bowed.

But Dumadora was deeply asleep on her scratchy bed mat, exhausted by her eighteen-hour day and the absence of her children. So exhausted that she had forgotten to push the treasured photograph back in its hiding place.

The first thing Rosa did was batter Dumadora awake with the heel of her shoe. Blood welled quickly from the puncture wounds on her face and neck and Dumadora woke quickly, shock and pain reducing her to quiet sobs.

The second thing the enraged woman did was to snatch the photograph from her maid's hand. Five botched abortions at the brothel had rendered Rosa barren and she particularly hated loving mothers, her own having sold her into the sex trade at eleven.

Very deliberately Rosa watched her maid's face as she tore the photograph in half, then half again and continued until tiny, indecipherable pieces littered the floor.

Her rage spent and immediately bored and thirsty, she left as quickly as she had come in search of water and a cigar.

Dumadora stared at the ruined picture in disbelief and shock and only then did she indeed fall to her knees in prayer. And there she stayed until dawn, her lips barely moving as she asked for the pain to stop and to find forgiveness in her heart.

After drinking a glass of water, frosted by cold, and a half Cohiba, smoked leisurely by the pool, her bronzed legs rippling in the water's shadows, Rosa went to bed. She gave no further thought to Dumadora's pain or her husband of only twelve hours.

She slept the sleep of innocents until the clock in the cool marble hallway ticked past midnight, and then she woke gently to a very faint clack clack. The noise was so quiet initially that Rosa thought it was the slap of Simon's feet on the marble as he made his way to the bathroom and she slipped back into a drowsy sleep.

When Rosa woke again, the sound was nearer, louder, and she sat up, eyes searching the room. clack clack. Whatever was making the noise was now in the bedroom, and when Rosa fumbled for the light switch, something bit her fingers, hard. She yelped and scrabbled backwards towards the headboard but the clack clack, clack clack marched onwards towards her. When the night clouds parted and the moon was allowed to briefly shine, Rosa was given enough light to see the five *Calaveras that floated grotesquely at the bottom of the bed and the one, with a bloody mouth, by her ear. The clack clack sound resonated as they bounced their teeth together in unison.

The sugar skulls' faces were tattooed with intricate, black markings and engraved with vibrant flowers, beautiful on any other night but not on this one and after they were done, Rosa had lost all her finger tips, the tops of her ears and her nose to the hunger of the Calaveras.

Afterwards, the bedclothes were burnt, the blood and other stains too deep, and Dumadora sighed as she tossed them into the fire because they were such good quality.

You might think that Dumadora would relish the downfall of Rosa Maria Martinez, her tormentor, but quite the opposite was true. Dumadora's devout nature and gentle spirit lent itself to caring for the traumatised Rosa. Washing her gently when she soiled herself, adjusting the nose mask to hide the deep scarring, and helping eat and drink because both those things are surprisingly difficult without fingers.

Rosa never spoke again and died weeks later in her sleep. She had too many pieces missing to ever be enjoyed again and Simon had tired of her quickly, as men like that are prone to do of broken things.

Dumadora left shortly afterwards for home, for the cool touch of the Amihan wind on her skin and for the soft arms of her children. Money always turned up when she needed it, the family was never short of food again and luck seemed to have landed permanently at their door.

Two days after Dumadora had returned to her homeland, Simon De Smet returned home late one evening, after a gorging on fine brandy, goose liver pate and willing women. He fell face down onto his soft bed and was asleep before eleven.

At one stroke past midnight, he woke and blamed the strange noises on his thumping head, and by the time he could make out the odd sounds clearly, it was too late.

clack clack
clack clack

Las Calaveras were hungry and they had come to feast on Simon's wickedness.

* Calaveras are the colourful and macabre sugar skulls that Latin countries use to honour their ancestors on the Day of The Dead.

S.A. Shields

Do you remember the first time we met?
You smiled a smile I could never forget.
You reached out your hand to mine,
and just liked that, I'd forgotten time.
Do you remember the first time our lips touched? I was
lost in your eyes, in your kiss,
every second in your arms was pure bliss.
Do you remember when we stayed up all night?
We told each other everything, our pasts, our fears, and
our dreams, until the sky was bright.
Do you remember the first time you told me
you loved me?
I knew by the look in your eyes it was true,
and from that moment on, all I wanted, all I could think
about was you.
Do you remember the first time you shouted at me?
Your voice was loud, so full of hate,
that I began to second guess if you were my fate.
Do you remember the second time you shouted at me?
You told me I was stupid, that I couldn't do anything
right,
then you left me upstairs in your bed, where tears
drenched my face all night.
Do you remember the man I fell for? The sweet, caring,
loving guy
who looked as though he couldn't hurt a fly?
I do, but now he's gone, and I'm a disgrace,
holding an ice pack to my cheek after you slapped me
across the face.

Do you remember when you cried?
You told me about your abusive dad and how you used to hide.
You promised you'd never hurt me again,
and I believed you, while carrying the blame.
Do you remember when things were going well?
You kept to your promise, and we found our way out of hell.
But soon enough, the monster came back,
and I found myself under your attack.
Do you remember when my body hit the floor?
You pushed me hard, even though you promised you wouldn't anymore.
I tried to get up, but when I did, I froze.
There was so much blood spilling from my nose.
Do you remember when you told me it was all my fault?
That I made you angry, that I made you sad.
That everything I did made you furiously mad.
You held me in your arms and I tried to feel for the man I fell in love with,
but he was gone, that man was a myth.
Do you remember when you had one too many beers? I was crying, screaming that I was sorry, curled up in a ball on the floor,
praying, please God, no more.
You kicked my stomach so hard I nearly heaved,
and the insults you kept spitting from your mouth, I started to believe.
Do you remember the first time I tried to escape? I ran for the door, but I didn't get far,
because you grabbed me by the hair and threw me into the breakfast bar.
You told me I was ugly, a useless whore,
that nobody else could have me, because I was yours.
Do you remember the second time I tried to escape?
It ended with rape.

I watched you zip your pants up, looking mighty
satisfied,
and then I realised the man I loved was no longer present
in your eyes.
Do you remember the day I finally ran away?
You called and texted me nonstop all day.
You promised that you would change.
I didn't know whether to believe you, or if you were
deranged.
Do you remember when I gave you too many second
chances? I met you at the beach, I sat waiting for you,
staring at the night sky,
only to find you lured me with a lie.
You told me you would kill me if I made a sound.
It was so dark, nobody was around.
I had no choice but to let you have your way,
and you let your brother join in to play.
Do you remember when you left me? All alone, locked
in my mind,
whatever was left of me, I couldn't find.
Now I sit here, writing this poem,
my pride, my life, stolen.
So I'll just stay here in my silence, and live in fear, in
pain,
just waiting for you to appear again.

Girl of my Dreams – A Saga of Failure

Adam Oster

Part 1:

I don't want to start this whole thing off on the wrong foot, but there's no better way of saying it. My high school days were probably different than yours. You see, I went to a boarding school. And no, it wasn't because my family was rich or anything. And it wasn't because I was that bad boy who got sent off to military school either. The truth is a lot less cool…and boring. It was a religious school and I come from a religious family.

Lack of excitement in backstory aside, it's not like my days were filled with prayer vigils and hymn singing. It was a high school. The main difference was: I just so happened to live there.

What this means is that I spent every waking hour with my classmates. Breakfast, lunch, dinner, and everything in between was with those same folks I would sit next to during Algebra, English, and Health classes. Obviously, there were some great aspects to this. For instance, I never had to ask my parents if I could head over to [insert friend's name here] to play video games. No, I just walked down to their room and knocked.

As I'm sure you've already guessed, there were some negative aspects to this arrangement as well. Since there was no home life, there really was no good way to keep everyone from knowing everything about you. You couldn't harbor a secret obsession with My Little Pony and get away with it. You couldn't go home and hug your mommy when you'd had a bad day. And if you liked someone, it was known by every single person in the entire school before lunch.

Speaking of which, the whole school consisted of less than one hundred people, freshmen, sophomores, juniors, and seniors included. So, when I say gossip traveled quickly, I'm not exaggerating. If someone caught a glimpse of your Superman underoos at 9am, you would be forever more known as SuperRoo by 10.

Needless to say, the stakes on sticking your neck out in my school were pretty large with even the most minor of high school offenses. I also just so happened to be a nerd, which meant I had to be cautious about everything. And the idea of me liking anyone out of my league, which was pretty much everyone, was an incredibly risky situation.

I spent a lot of time ignoring any feelings I might have had for anyone. The stakes were too high. If I came out as a contender too early, while still appearing to be nothing more than a nerd, I could have risked ending my career as a boyfriend in the school early. And as a young awkward teenage male, well, I really wanted to be a boyfriend. Well, maybe not a boyfriend as much as a boy with a girl he could, you know, touch and stuff.

But I did finally step out on a limb and officially entered the dating game during my second year. A girl I had met in summer camp a few years prior was a freshman and we instantly hit it off. We started dating shortly after the school year began.

Things were going pretty well, I think. We hit a bit of a snafu when I found out we were second cousins, but I'm sure we could have even made it through that if it hadn't been for the fact that this was the precise same time when I met The Girl of My Dreams.

I still remember the first time I laid eyes on The Girl of My Dreams. Well, considering she was best friends with my girlfriend of the time and I had been dating this girl for a couple months already, it probably wasn't the first time I had actually seen The GOMD, but it was the first time I remember noticing her. So perhaps it would be better to state that I still remember the first time I noticed the GOMD. It's hazy. I don't remember it quite like it was yesterday. But it was a life-changing moment.

Okay, life-changing is probably going a bit overboard, I'll admit it. Look, it meant something at the time, I'm sure. And it led me down a long path of unrequited love. A path that is causing me to tell you this story in the first place, so if you're going to get all bogged down in the semantics of my exposition, it might be time to turn away now, because I can assure you it ain't getting any better from here on out. If you leave now, you'll get a simple story of "Nerdy Boy Finds Cute Chick Attractive", as opposed to the truth of what would happen.

So, where was I? Oh yeah…

There she was, in the arms of her boyfriend of the time, me standing awkwardly beside my girlfriend of the time. Then we locked eyes. I swear I was looking at her eyes.

"Hi," she said, as she rolled a wad of green chewing gum around on her tongue.

"Hi," I said, trying to find a way to show that my current relationship wasn't very serious, which was difficult because Current Girlfriend was holding my hand like I might run away at any second.

"Nice shoes," she replied, pointing to my boring black flip flops.

I attempted my best version of a cool shrug and stammered, "I like your hair." It was red. Well, reddish anyways.

"Yeah? I was thinking about going blonde next."

"Cool," I shrugged again. Was I shrugging too much? Probably. How much shrugging can you do before cool turns into twitchy?

"Hey," CG cut in. I blinked rapidly, suddenly remembering she was there. She wrapped her arms around me and began talking. I'm not sure if this was a move of claiming territory or simply an awkward high school display of affection. "Do you two want to come to the mall with us later today? We were thinking about watching a movie."

"Um, yeah, I'd love to go." I caught myself mid-shrug, figuring the non-committal response would be enough to show I was being cool about the whole thing.

"Uh, of course you're coming," CG said with a great deal of unanticipated sassiness. "I was asking GOMD and HB [Her Boyfriend] if they wanted to come with us."

"Oh," I shrugged again, this time not even aware I was doing it. "Yeah, I know. I was just making a joke, you big dummy." I lightly punched her in the shoulder. She looked at me angrily. I cowered in fear.

"I think we're going out to pick out some new jeans for HB," GOMD replied. "Not sure we'll be able to make the movie, but maybe we'll see you out there."

"Sounds like a plan," I said with a wink and a finger-gun. I instantly gave myself a mental pummeling as I recognized I was doing it.

GOMD stepped closer to me and looked deep in my eyes. Her head cocked quizzically. I found my heart racing in response to this sudden attention.

Then she said them. The life-altering words which would forever imprint this moment upon me.

"Do you know you have a lisp?"

Part 2:

Can I first say that no other person in my entire life has ever pointed out my inability to articulate sibilants? Not one. None before that moment and none after. So, not only was I blindsided by this idea that I might have a speech impediment, but it also came out of the girl I had just put all of my future plans for admiration behind. I remember spending the entire rest of the day walking around the mall and saying words with an S in them. I very quickly realized she was right. Or, had she just cursed me with the inability to speak clearly, seeing as I had been completely oblivious to this fact until that very moment? Fifteen years, I had been unaware of my own sigmatism. It seems probable that it was a new development.

Side note: Words like sibilants, sigmatism, and lisp should not be attached to this particular ailment.

Needless to say, The GOMD had already made a lasting impression on me. There hasn't been a day since that one where I haven't been acutely aware of how my extra-large tongue likes to work against me.

In spite of this life-changing moment, things actually did begin to look up shortly after it occurred. Things between me and CG ended around the same time The GOMD was freed from the tyranny of that guy I still hate. We were both single. And we had started this odd daily ritual of hugging each other upon first sight (something I still don't fully understand, but don't regret). AND a mutual friend invited us both to hang at her house for the upcoming three-day weekend.

I was over the moon. It would be just the three of us, all hanging out at the same house, for three whole days. Since it was me and two girls, I knew this had nothing but "Amazing Weekend" written all over it. It had to. Right?

As the fated moment grew near, I became more and more eager, knowing this would be the time where I would finally be able to make my move. Knowing she was obviously working toward that same end goal. She had to have been, right? How else would this amazing weekend opportunity of awesomeness have come about, if she hadn't been the one orchestrating it?

A few days later, I made it down to breakfast, something I rarely did due to how early 6am was (and still is) and found an open spot available next to The GOMD. I'd love to say that I merely sat drooling obsessively over her throughout the meal, but seriously, I wasn't that pathetic, just smitten. However, even the power of The GOMD couldn't win out over my need for sleep, especially since this was a year or two before I discovered (and then immediately became addicted to) coffee.

I can't even pretend there was some sort of cute awkward conversation that occurred between us, because more than likely I stared at the wall as I slowly attempted to eat the multi-colored circles of cereal I most often ate when I did make it to breakfast. Seriously, 6am was (and is) too early.

There really is only one reason I remember this moment existed at all, and that is that this was the morning she handed me a note (you know, those handwritten things folded up into impossibly tiny shapes with doodles all over the outside) and asked if I would deliver it to a classmate of mine when I returned to the boys' dormitory.

The early morning didn't help anything, but my first reaction was nothing. Without question, I accepted the task, being the helpful guy I am. It wasn't until the meal was over and I had made the walk back up the hill to where I slept that my brain started questioning the activities of the past thirty minutes.

"Why is she writing notes to someone else?" I muttered to myself in confusion. "I know we're not dating, but this weekend…"

"Actually," I thought, "maybe that's exactly what this is about. Maybe she wants to check to see if my friend has any details about how I felt about the weekend."

As I walked up the stairs to my room, my heart began beating out of my chest.

"In my hands, I could be holding the very proof I need that she's interested in me!" My brain was in overdrive.

I needed to know. There were so many variables. I had kept my infatuation a secret, meaning that although the person this note was intended to was someone I might have considered a friend, he definitely wouldn't be aware of my attraction. And should this be a question to know if she was going to get anything from me over the course of the weekend, well, he might answer no.

He most definitely would answer no and I would have lost the very opportunity I needed to actually start this relationship I had been working on trying to start for so long—

Of course, on the other side of the coin, what if I was wrong? What if this really was a note about math homework or something, and not about me at all? I can't open up to my friend about this interest I have only for the note to be about homework. It could ruin everything if news of my love gets out early. Everything!

A struggle began building inside me. There were too many things up in the air, too many variables that could lead to absolute ruin. I knew it was wrong, but I had only one option.

I slipped into my room, closed the door, and huddled in my closet as I fumbled to open the piece of paper and find out what the note was about.

"*Dear Person Who Used to be Adam's Friend,*
I wish I was able to spend the weekend with you

instead of going to Other Friend's house. It's going to be so boring there---"

I didn't need to read any further. My heart fell.

Sure, it was true, we hadn't really moved onto the exciting part of our relationship yet. I like to let things percolate a bit before I move in for the strike, so, you know, there was a lot of groundwork being laid. But this seemed like a message of death.

I immediately told myself that it wasn't as bad as it looked.

Until I realized that she was comparing a weekend with me to a weekend with PWUTBAF.

What was up with that? I had never even seen them together! Had they been going around behind my back? Did he not know that she was the girl of MY dreams?

I wanted to give PWUTBAF an earful. I wanted to give The GOMD an earful.

Of course, neither of them even knew I was interested.

And more importantly, I shouldn't even have been reading this note.

More importantly, if The GOMD were to find out that I was reading a note she had written for someone else, it would certainly ruin what little we had going for us already.

I carefully folded the note up to as close of an approximation of its initial folding as possible and placed it under PWUTBAF's door.

Part 3:

Not much changed immediately following the moment with the note. I skipped out on the planned weekend. Something about it seemed tainted, which I'm sure doesn't come as a surprise. And I wasn't too certain I could keep quiet about the note.

I attempted to put some space between us, which was difficult, considering the daily hug ritual and how the daily life in our school generally worked. I mean, we slept in buildings that were only a hundred yards apart from each other. Space wasn't really in the cards.

Summer was approaching soon, which might offer the needed opportunity for distance. She lived in Minnesota, while I lived in South Carolina. I figured that a summer apart might be just what this relationship needed in order to reboot. I knew it was a long shot, but, well, you know how infatuation goes, right?

Then, one day, out of the blue, she came running toward me with an enormous smile covering her face. She wrapped her arms around me and held on tight. Yeah, we had our daily hugs, but this was different. It was like she was excited to see me or something. Had my plan really worked? I wasn't even sure I had been able to enact it yet.

"You'll never guess what just happened," she exclaimed.

"What?" I said.

"My dad just got offered a job in Columbia!"

"What?" I repeated.

"My dad just—"

"No, I heard you, just…wow. Really?"

"Yep. He just told me on the phone less than five minutes ago."

"In South Carolina?"

"Yeah, dummy. Of course."

"That's—"

"Awesome, right? Now we'll be able to spend all summer together. Isn't that just amazing?"

"Yeah," I agreed. And it was. Sure, it went completely against my plans for getting some distance to allow the heart to grow fonder or whatever, but a whole summer together? Without all the rest of these people from school around? Without PWUTBAF around… This was obviously a sign.

"He hasn't taken the job yet," she added. "But how cool would it be if he did?"

"Yeah," I shrugged. Just go with it. Shrugging was my thing now. "That would be cool, I guess."

"Yeah, right?" she smiled and pulled me in for another hug.

He did take the job and I spent the rest of the school year on cloud nine. She would be moving right away at the start of the summer. Even better than that, she would be living just slightly over a mile away from my parents. It's crazy, right? Almost unbelievably crazy, right?

Believe me, that's exactly what I thought.

All doubts I had regarding the Fates which would bring me and The GOMD together were completely dissolved. This truth was unquestionable. We were meant to be together.

The rest of the school year flew by like a dream. I remember spending hours sitting out under the spring sun talking about how our summers could be entwined. She would ask me at length about all the things there were to do there. I would sit and wonder how I could possibly have gotten so lucky.

And then summer came. Things started off with a bang. I met her parents the day they moved in and we immediately hit things off. Her mother would tell me how my hugs were the best she'd ever had. Her father told me I was the only person he was going to allow to drive his daughter anywhere. Look at that, I had already nailed the 'meeting the parents' part of the job description.

Even better, I had a job working at a grocery store and she got a job working at a fast food restaurant which just so happened to be located on the way.

Every day I would stop by on my way to work and

buy lunch. I told her it was where I had always stopped to eat. Didn't want her to think I was going too far out of my way to see her, right? Gotta keep it cool. To be honest, I had never eaten there before. The milkshakes I told her were the best you could find were, at best, okay. There were much better places for me to eat a greasy lunch, but that didn't stop me from eating there every day for the summer.

And every day, as I made my way down the road to see her, I would consider how I could make that day the one. The one where I would finally end all this foolishness and make our relationship official.

There was only one possible way to seal the deal, of course. A kiss.

"Perhaps I'll pull her over the front counter as she hands me my milkshake, our lips will lock, and things will be irreversibly changed."

"It's raining out. What's more romantic than pulling up to the drive-thru window and reaching through in the pouring rain to share that first kiss?"

And each time I left to continue on my way to work, I would mentally berate myself for not following through, visualizing the multitude of moments where I could have made things happen, but ultimately couldn't pull the trigger.

Every day was the same. Except the one where my visualizing the prior few minutes caused me not to visualize the present.

WHAM! A car plowed into the front of my parents' van when I attempted to take a left onto a busy highway, apparently unaware of the vehicle headed in my direction. In shock, I watched it hit another car headed in the opposite direction.

No one was hurt. I promise this was the first thing I looked into.

All I remember is how I sat on the sidewalk and

feared. I feared that the GOMD could see me and my traveling difficulties, considering how my vehicle sat immediately in front of her eating establishment. I feared my traffic violation might end her father's faith in me. I feared that this one moment had ruined everything.

Part 4:

As you might have expected, the accident didn't play much into anything. I'm not sure my status as approved chauffeur changed at all and I'm also not sure The GOMD even made any real reference to the accident, outside of noting how her and her fellow co-workers had seen that something had happened and were concerned about anyone getting hurt.

Again, I want to note that no one was injured, at least not seriously. Although I still can't imagine how.

But this is about me and The GOMD. And when it comes down to that, the next piece of important knowledge is that I actually got a date! Like, a real date, or at least that's how I saw it, you know, at the movie theater and everything.

It was a pretty big deal in my mind. Yet, in reality, here's how the actual act of getting the date probably went:

"Hey, there's this movie that I kinda want to see. Want to go with me?" That was me.

"Yeah, sure, I'm free on Friday."

"Great!"

So, the day of the movie arrived and we decided to hit up the food court at the mall in order to eat a little something before the flick started. Fast food is always the way to a woman's heart, right?

As we sat eating our sandwiches, we had the chance to catch up a bit. My life had become a bit more hectic after the accident, due to things like having to take a defensive driving course and making sure I could get to work without the vehicle I had been using. I hadn't really seen much of her throughout most of the summer by this point.

Somehow, the conversation transitioned over to something of a more personal nature.

"I just wish I could find a nice guy who is also cute, you know?" Is it not obvious that this is her talking? "My sisters always get the cute guys. I always end up with the ugly jerks."

At this point, I felt quite tongue-tied. I'm not saying I'm beautiful or anything. I think I'm about a foot too short for that. But I don't think I'm unattractive. And if there's one thing my track record says for me, it's that I'm nice…possibly too nice when it comes to my interactions with women.

Instead, my response was something more akin to, "Really? I'd think you would find all sorts of attractive guys."

And then she shrugged off the comment and we continued on our merry way to the movie.

Don't get me wrong, I totally recognized the possibility that the comment about finding a nice cute guy could be a lead in for me. Even knowing that I was suffering from a bad case of being stuck in the friend zone, I saw the possibility there and I prayed for it to be true.

Going into the theater, I knew this might be my one chance. Theaters are a pretty spectacular place for getting things started. There you are, just sitting alone in the dark, right next to each other. There are all sorts of possibilities. I set my sights low. I figured that if I could just get her hand in mine, everything would fall into place the way it should.

So, I put my mind to the task. The movie started, I

made sure to leave her the arm rest. What better way to get the hand in grabbing position than to have it on the rest, right? She…well, she didn't take it.

Well, not right away.

I kept watching the damned arm rest and when she finally did take it, I had already lost my nerve. If she had any interest in me grabbing her hand so she could learn how intensely sweaty my palms were (it's a medical condition, I promise), then she definitely would have put her hand there right off the bat, right?

So, there it was, just sitting there for me to grab. I couldn't do it.

Want to know what I actually did?

It's embarrassing, really.

I mean, like, really embarrassing.

Considering I couldn't grab her hand and all.

I'm really not sure I should even tell you.

Okay, fine…I put my head on her shoulder.

It really probably doesn't seem that bad in that framework. Sure, I was touching her. It was mildly intimate. But here's the thing. We were in old school theater seats. Those arm rests didn't go up. The only way in which I could put my head on her shoulder was through the most obscene position possible.

And I'm sure she noticed.

I was practically horizontal in my seat, all for the purposes of copping out on a handhold and putting my head on her shoulder.

The disappointment was palpable. But I had made the move already. I couldn't really get out of it easily without appearing disinterested, right? She had accepted the move. Leaned into it even. But there was no possible way that she saw this as anything more than a pathetic attempt at friendliness.

And I still didn't grab the damned hand.

Part 5:

Alright, so the movie thing didn't turn out as bad as I had feared. I had managed to show her in some way that I was interested in her and she hadn't immediately turned me down. Things were looking okay.

Not great, but okay.

The end of summer was quickly approaching and I knew my options were disappearing fast. If I didn't somehow manage to seal the deal before summer was over, she would be back in the world of people she knew, back where her options for mates were much greater. And I would be back to being nothing but a friend. If even that, after the movie fiasco.

Here's where I managed my greatest feat. I'm still not even sure how it worked out. I'm guessing she was more instrumental in its happening than I was. But, we finally decided, a few weeks before school started, to sneak out of our houses after our families had gone to sleep and meet up at the football field that was the precise midpoint between our homes.

I was in!

There was no doubt about it. I! WAS! IN!

Here was the plan. After our parents were down and out, we would hit each other up through instant messenger stating as much and then head down to the field.

It was simple. So simple.

There was absolutely no possible way in which this wouldn't work out without me landing a girlfriend by the end of it. Or at least a story I could be proud of.

The time came and we were off. That walk to the field, which was only about half a mile, had my heart racing like it had never done before. She was so definitely into me. There wasn't a chance she wasn't. She wanted this. She wanted to meet at the football field after dark. What other possible choice could there be?

Only question now was, how would I start it? Would I just start the whole thing off with a big kiss, or would I move in slowly, perhaps a hug that led to a handheld walk around the nearby woods?

Let's just say that I had countless itineraries laid out for how I could cause this to progress.

Not a single one of them happened.

Here's what did happen:

We got there. We greeted each other with the standard hug. We sat down at the bleachers and started talking.

One of us (I'm sure it was her) suggested we sit in the middle of the field to check out the stars. We did.

We wrestled.

Okay, I should probably focus on that a bit. We literally wrestled. We were rolling around in the grass on top of each other.

Let that bounce around in your brain a bit. We were rolling around in the grass. And it was nothing more than flirtatious goofiness. Nothing.

She managed to use the wrestling to get herself in a position where she was actually straddling me, with me lying on my back on the grass. The image is burnt into my mind. This was the moment. Out of all the hundreds, nay thousands, of moments I had seen where I could seal this whole thing with a kiss, this was the one. I remember so few things about my attempts to garner The GOMD's attention as vividly as this one precise moment.

The moment where we stopped wrestling and just looked into each other's eyes. I swear I was looking at her eyes.

And I remember absolutely nothing else about our time on the field. Not a single thing.

Not because, you know, cool things happened and I just don't want to mention them. No, because I didn't make the one single obvious move that should have happened right at that very second. I chickened the hell out and, well, there was no point in my brain even operating any more. It was over.

I do believe that our time out ended quite shortly after that moment. We both went our separate ways, probably enjoying another one of those stupid hugs.

And I was at home.

Behind my computer.

Cursing myself for my damned insecurities in something that even I knew was a certain thing. I mean, it was certain, right? Obviously the whole reason I chickened out was because I was still afraid of being rejected. Maybe I had noticed something, something that said that this was just one of the weirdest events in Friend Zone history.

Then a little window popped up on my computer screen. A message from The GOMD.

"Was it just me, or were you expecting something more to happen tonight, too?"

Part 6:

I had failed. This much I knew. School started back up and all I could think about was the fact that I had somehow completely and utterly failed in the one goal I had for myself for those three months.

And now I had to go back to a school year knowing that news would get around.

I felt pathetic.

Then I got a bright idea. You see, my birthday happens to be right at the start of the school year. The first weekend of school, that particular year. And I knew just what I could do to make things happen.

It wasn't uncommon for students to rent out a hotel

room and throw a party for their birthdays. A chaperone was to be present at all times, of course. And I knew that if I were to throw a party, this would be the exact moment in which I could express my love for The GOMD and since it was my birthday, she would have to be willing to forgive my failures over the course of the summer and give it a try. After all, I knew she was interested. What else could that message have meant, right? I'll admit right now that I was a little too naïve to even consider the idea that she was just looking for a fling.

So, the party was set and since it was the start of the school year, it quickly became something of note around the school. I invited every single person I could and made sure The GOMD promised me she would be there.

And although there was the whole standard sitcom process of waiting until the last second to arrive, she did make it. And, just like in those sitcoms, she almost as quickly decided that she had other things to do.

I stopped her. In my first act of almost a year of being in love with this girl, I actually used some willpower and actually made her stay for a minute and talk to me.

"So, um, I know I kind of screwed up that whole thing at the field," I said, forcing myself to actually be honest here.

"Don't worry about it. It just wasn't meant to be."

"But I want it to be. I was just scared or something that you didn't like me back."

"Don't worry about it, Adam. It's all in the past."

"But, GOMD, I don't want it to be in the past, I want it to be in the future."

"Yeah," she replied in a way that showed she had absolutely no idea of how to respond to such a plea.

"I'm just saying that I'd like to start dating. I really like you."

"Oh."

"So, will you?"

"Will I what?"

"Date me? You know, like boyfriend and girlfriend? We don't have to call it that or anything if you don't want—"

"I don't know, Adam. I had just—"

"Can't we just give it a try?"

"I really don't know. School just started again, things are all up in the air, I really just don't—"

"Okay, maybe in a couple weeks then, when you get more situated? I can wait a couple weeks."

"For me? Why would you want to wait a couple weeks for me?"

"Because I like you."

"Yeah, you said that."

"I'm just saying, maybe we can hold it off, but still give it a try."

"I just don't know, Adam."

"You want to think about it?"

"I guess so, sure. Why don't we think about it?"

"Great!"

"Okay, I've got to go, okay?"

"Okay."

"Happy birthday."

"Thanks!"

And that was, quite possibly, the last I talked to her in any real capacity for years.

Don't get me wrong, I don't blame her a bit. That conversation was quite possibly the most awkward conversation I have ever had and I've had hundreds of awkward conversations.

It wasn't just awkward because of the words and the failed emotions going on. No, you see, she had arrived at the party with PWUTBAF. Part of the reason I was so forward with her for the first time ever is that I could see how obvious it was that a relationship was blooming between them already and I had no choice but to make my move.

Another part of the reason it was so awkward, was because it was happening in the middle of a party in a small hotel room, with all of my friends watching...

Part 7:

My relationship history is filled with moments like these, moments where I would latch onto someone and be completely incapable of telling them how I feel about them. That's not to say I didn't have my fair share of relationships. Heck, I'm very happily married right now with three kids and, well, things just keep looking up on that front.

But me and The GOMD were just not meant to be. I've accepted that. This isn't a story trying to tell you how maybe someday Fate will step in and make things better. No. This is a story telling you that sometimes Fate just wants to play with your heart in order to show you how absolutely pathetic you truly are.

Of course, the story didn't end at the birthday party. Shortly after that event, I did get myself into a bit of a relationship, one that lasted for years, one that I was certain would end in marriage, even. But you know how those high school deals go.

Yet, for years the idea of this moment I had shared with The GOMD, a moment that could have changed the course of my life, stuck with me. And there were many times where I thought things might still work out. We did, after all, still have our summers together.

But things were never quite the same.

Then, suddenly, my high school relationship ended, years after I was out of high school. And at the same time I heard she was getting divorced. I'm not an opportunist, I promise. I didn't think that I could use this terrible moment in her life in order to live out some high school fantasy of my own. Well, I mean, there was probably some part of me who considered that, let's be honest, but seriously, I felt bad for her. I promise.

By this point, I had moved to Wisconsin and she was living full time in South Carolina. On a whim, powered heavily by a few bottles of Wisconsin's finest, I called her up one night, figuring we had similar woes to commiserate over.

And it was really awesome. We hadn't really talked in years, nothing really since that night on the football field. Yet, somehow, things immediately picked up again. It was pretty great. We talked for hours, the entire time both of us drinking our cares away. Things felt like they were actually going to go somewhere of worth.

And as luck would have it, I was destined to head home for my sister's wedding a few weeks after that talk.

My hopes weren't high, but there was definitely a feeling of Fate coming into play again.

There was an additional element at play, however; one that Fate might have had a hand in as well. The High School Sweetheart was in the wedding. And we had bought our plane tickets before the breakup, meaning we would be spending a lot of time together.

I still remember the first moment of seeing GOMD when I got to the church for the wedding. We had a lovely little chat. She even tried convincing me to move home again.

By this point, I had already spent several hours cramped up in a plane beside HSS and my mind was on other things.

Other things which led to finally getting that kiss on that football field. Just with the wrong girl.

That's right. As with so many failed relationships

before me, I made the mistake of going home with the bridesmaid who had already told me she wasn't interested.

And the birthday following that? The HSS called me up to go out and have dinner together, just the two of us.

So she could tell me she had been seeing other guys.

My life's pretty cyclical like that.

Thank God, I found the woman who would become my wife. We've stayed away from all football fields so far, outside of the gift shop at Lambeau.

Rain

Angelika Rust

Patter, patter, goes the rain against the window. Tiny droplets, hitting the pane, running down, coalescing on the sill outside. Condensation wets the frame from the inside. The view is misted over.

She's been standing there for hours, painting circles on the breath-frosted glass. There's sunshine, somewhere behind those gray clouds.

He puts his bottle down and burps. "Well, it's not gonna let up. Someone's gotta walk the dog. You or me?"

"You," she says, without turning her head, and her fingers keep tracing patterns he doesn't see. "If I do it, I won't come back."

i think i need a shower

Bradley Darewood

the soft
caress
makes my mind explode
(that tantalizing touch)
a roaring ocean in my ears
swallowing my every thought in it's endless depths
there is only you
(goosebumps on my skin)
i can feel your heartbeat
throbbing
with me
throbbing
warm like the womb
i close my eyes into your kiss
an oblivion of blackness
a darkness so inviting
i plunge
(your fingernails on my back)
love and lust are one
drenched in a tsunami of ecstasy
my ears tremble from the warmth of your breath
as you whisper…

"Shit, I forgot...
I'm on my period."

Down The Drain

Ken Alexopoulos

The anger I had cultivated to that point faded with the realization that I could have altered the course of events if I had merely voiced the issue prior to it ever coming to a head. Was it hate? No, it was much deeper than that. The pain and suffering that coursed through my veins held no malice, but the traces of betrayal festered as a constant throb rather than a tumultuous loathing. It was the most peculiar sensation that I had ever known and infinitely more mysterious than any carnal act. I knew it to be something described in print, yet the precise context and use of this foreign melancholy proved elusive.

Ten minutes had flown past without a word, the space between us an ocean of lost opportunity and the ebb and flow of silence crashed against the borders with the gravity of a dying star.

Just then, with no warning or means to defend against the onslaught, I farted. The air began to taste like last night's chili and the chair, composed of metal and cheap wood, felt soggy beneath my flank.

"Ah, fuck..." she heaved, "...I can't believe you've done this."

Blood rushed to my cheeks in an instantaneous response. The cloud carried the mixture of ingredients with such strength, such potency, that I could count the multitude of jalapeno peppers based on a minor shift in the wind. A stream of mud found its way along my thigh and inched toward my ankle, calling forth the bacterial decay and organic refuse as it began to collect in a widening puddle.

"I am so, so sorry..." I spoke, although the time for an apology had long since passed. I knew I should have taken her offer on the free drawer. It seemed both late and unlikely that the opportunity would still be available.

"Oh my god," she shouted as tears formed in the corners of her eyes, "it smells so bad!"

"I'll clean it up," I offered and pulled myself from the vacuum seal caused by a combination of my own fecal matter and the wetness of the wood, now stained a deeper brown. The act only served to worsen matters as a loud sucking noise reverberated through the living room and forced what little stayed within my bowels to extract itself onto the floor through my pants.

"Why are you doing this?!" she cried, her palms covering her face as she fought off the urge to retch and refused to bear witness to the despicable display.

Bent over and drenched in my own waste and anal expungement, I removed my shirt only to find that the trail of soft copper had made its way along the small of my spine, effectively ruining any plans I may have had to use the fabric as a wash-cloth. "It's not my fault!" I screamed, my voice high-pitched and frantic as I tried to void my stomach along with the already evident mass of digested fibers.

The relationship had officially gone down the toilet shortly afterwards, but at least something that night had made it.

For the Love of Cats and Dogs

S.A. Shields

Tracie

Tracie had the most horrid feeling of uncertainty in her stomach. Her friend and neighbour for the past fifteen years, Marion, worried her. At first, she figured her friend was going through a phase. A late midlife crisis at fifty. But every time she went into Marion's house, the clutter seemed to have grown.

There was stuff everywhere. And not just random stuff. Cat stuff. The walls were covered in pictures of kittens and cats of all different shapes, sizes and breeds. Even the cushions had cats printed on them. Ornaments. Lampshades. Magnets. Cups. Plates. You name it, there was a cat on it. Tracie didn't have the heart to tell her friend she thought she may need professional help, that the obsession she had was unhealthy, and that other people on the street referred to her as the crazy cat lady.

Marion

Marion cradled her cup of warm tea, listening to the purring of Puddles, her life and joy, as he slept on her lap, and also listening to Tracie's nonsense advice.

"I hope you don't think I'm being out of order, love," Tracie continued. "I just want you to find someone. Wouldn't you be happier if you had someone to share your life with?"

Marion's lips curved at the sides as she popped her tea back onto the coffee table, atop of the adorable kitten coaster she bought last week. "What makes you think I'm not happy? Besides, I do have someone to share my life with."

Tracie rolled her eyes. "A cat isn't someone to share your life with."

"What do you suggest then, hmm? That I find another man like my cheating ex-husband?"

Tracie ran a hand through her short, frizzy hair, which was starting to grey. "Of course not. But you know, not all men are the same."

As much as Marion did want to meet someone, she'd tried the whole love thing numerous times, and it always went west. Wayne, the first man she briefly dated after the divorce, ended up being allergic to cats. Even though she liked him, a man whose eyes watered and nose itched around Puddles just wouldn't do. It wasn't practical long term.

Then there was Kenneth. He loved Puddles as much as Marion did, but the day he left the back door open to almost let Puddles outside, signalled the end of him. What would she have done if Puddles had escaped? He'd never been outside without Marion, and that was the way Marion wanted to keep it. The outside world was too dangerous.

"I'd better be off." Tracie got to her feet. "David's flying in from New York tonight."

David was Tracie's only son, who'd made a good life for himself as a lawyer to all the top celebrities. Marion felt an ache in her chest. She'd always wanted a child, but complications with her ovaries meant she would never be able to conceive. And her ex-husband never fancied adopting. At least Puddles somewhat filled the place of a child.

Marion

It was a beautiful, sunny Sunday afternoon in Somerset. The cool breeze, which brought some relief from the heat, smelt of seaweed, and the local stretch of beach was lively, mostly full of kids and half naked men and women sunbathing. Marion was taking Puddles for his usual walk, on the cat leash. Arriving at her local café, she took a seat under a shaded area and placed Puddles on her lap. "Let me guess," said the young waitress. "A black coffee and some milk for Puddles."

"Yes, please, Kerry." As Marion stroked her cat's warm, black, shiny coat, she noticed a man at the table across from her. He was staring at her over the top of his newspaper. She gave a small smile before looking away. But it wasn't long before she found herself looking at him again, and this time, he smiled and folded his newspaper on the table. When he got to his feet and walked toward her, Marion's stomach tingled.

"Can't say I've ever seen someone with a cat at a café before."

Marion's cheeks burned under the force of his handsome smile. "Well, there's a first time for everything."

"There certainly is. May I join you? Or are you waiting for your boyfriend?"

A giggle slipped her lips, the kind of giggle she hadn't heard from her mouth in years. "You must be joking," she replied, placing her free hand on her chest. "I'm a bit old for that kind of terminology."

The man took it upon himself to slide a chair out and take a seat. "You don't look a day over twenty."

She flapped her hand, cheeks burning again as this stranger made her feel like a giddy school girl. "Oh, stop. You're too kind."

"What's your name?"

"Marion."

The man extended a hand. "Graham."

Nice name, Marion thought. Her eyes took in his features. Brown hair with a hint of grey at the sides. Deep blue eyes, and grey stubble covering his jaw. She shifted in her seat as Puddles meowed and dug his nails into her lap. "You look familiar…have we met?"

"I doubt it. I would remember meeting someone as beautiful as you." A dimple formed at the left side of his mouth, and it was from that moment, that Marion found herself in love.

Tracie

This was an improvement. Last week when she saw Marion, she was worried for her friend's sanity, but now she looked like a different person. There was a sparkle in her previously lifeless eyes, and Puddles was nowhere to be seen, properly locked away in the kitchen. Marion was sitting on the couch, telling Tracie all about Graham, a structural engineer she'd met at the local coffee shop.

"I'm so happy, Tracie. I really didn't believe I could be in love again, but Graham is something else. I can't wait for you to meet him."

Tracie was relieved. But that relief didn't last long. Low and behold, the following week, Tracie heard a commotion coming from next door, mostly the sound of Marion screeching. She took off her pinafore and hung it on the kitchen door. Her chocolate cake would have to wait. She needed to make sure Marion was okay.

After knocking for five minutes, she was about to walk around the back of the house, when the front door flew open, making Tracie startle. Marion's face was bright red, her eyebrows so drawn together Tracie was afraid they might overlap. "He's got a dog!" Marion roared. "He's got a damn Rottweiler!"

A tall man hurried behind her, who Tracie assumed was Graham. "Marion! Calm down. It's not that big a deal."

"Not that big a deal! I can't have a dog around Puddles." She turned to Graham. "Have you lost your mind? Get out!"

"Mazzy-"

Tracie stood aside. "Don't you Mazzy me! I said get out, now!"

Graham stormed through the door and down the driveway. She watched as he jumped into his Mercedes and slammed the door.

"Marion, what on earth is going on?"

Tracie followed Marion inside, fiddling with her fingernails as Marion stomped around the kitchen, cleaning up in the loudest manner, slamming cupboard doors and throwing dishes into the sink, so hard Tracie was sure something had smashed.

"Marion," Tracie started, but was cut short by Marion's sobs.

"He's got a dog. He was going to move in…I-I knew he was too good to be true." Marion fell to the kitchen floor, burying her face in a tea towel.

Anyone would think it was the end of the world, Tracie thought. She didn't remember Marion being this upset when she found out her husband was having an affair. The woman was making an apocalypse out of something so small. This was the kind of situation that would take away anyone's ability to say something. So, Tracie said nothing. She sat crossed legged in front of her friend, on the cold kitchen tiles, and waited for Marion to calm down.

Two weeks later
Graham

He couldn't believe his perfect start to a relationship had almost been broken by the fact he had a dog. Either way, he wasn't going to get rid of Dodger. He'd had the Rottweiler since he was just a pup. Saved him from a puppy farm, where his fate was most certainly a gas tank.

What he did do, though, was compromise. Lucky for him, Marion agreed to let Graham move in, as long as Dodger lived outside in a kennel. He hated the compromise, but was sure in time Marion would learn to love Dodger the way he did. And maybe one day she would get rid of that stupid cat.

He couldn't tell her he hated cats. And when he said hated, he meant it. He despised everything about them. The way they lazed around doing absolutely nothing, the way their tails stuck up to show off their disgusting arseholes, and the way they trampled all over you as if it was their god given right.

You can't train a cat. They won't go away when you tell them to, they won't sit, give a paw, lie down, roll over, play dead. Nothing. And that purring. Yep, he hated cats. And especially Puddles. The damn thing got more attention than he did. But Graham hoped that by him moving in, he would be able to free Marion from her awful cat obsession. She would soon become a dog person with him and Dodger around.

Marion

Disgusting, absolutely disgusting, Marion thought as she scooped up poop from the lawn. How did she end up having this job? She agreed to let Dodger live in the garden, not clean up after him. That's the thing about dogs, they poop wherever they feel like it, and they don't even clean up after themselves. At least Puddles has the decency to bury his business when he's finished.

Marion looked Dodger in the eyes. "Yes, you keep wagging your tail and slobbering whilst I clean up your droppings, you filthy animal."

Dodger plonked his bottom on the grass, letting go of a little whine and bowing his head slightly. It was then Marion felt a tad guilty. She rolled her eyes and patted the dog cautiously on the head, as a peace making of sorts. She figured as long as Dodger was going to be here, they would have to get along. They didn't necessarily have to like each other, though.

Graham

Everything was going perfect. He and Marion had just finished off a beautiful vegetable stir-fry that he had cooked for them that evening, washing it down with a glass of the best red wine he could afford. His palms were sweating as he stared into Marion's hazel eyes, watching her finish off the last bit of wine in her glass.

Please don't choke on it, he thought.

Marion gasped and her eyes shifted to the bottom of the glass. "Is-is this what…what I think it is?"

Graham took the napkin off his lap, walked around the table and knelt on one knee. "Marion, from the moment I met you, I knew we would spend our lives together. Will you do me the immense honour of being my wife?"

Tracie

Tracie jumped out of her seat when she heard Marion

scream. Running to the front door, her feet nearly slipped on the wet grass as she hurried to Marion's house "Marion!" she shouted, banging her fist on the door. "Marion!"

The door flew open, and Tracie stood still, heart racing, waiting to hear that the dog had a secret litter of puppies somewhere, and preparing herself to console Marion for the rest of the evening.

"We're getting married!" she cried.

Tracie let go a huge breath of relief. "Oh, Marion! Congratulations, sweetheart." She embraced her, praising the lord that her friend had finally found someone, and she wouldn't have to worry about her anymore.

Graham

Graham was sitting in the living room, sprawled out on the couch with Dodger curled up in front of the TV. Marion seemed to be content with the fact Dodger was in Puddles' place. She was all too busy staring at the diamond ring on her finger. Tonight was the perfect moment, after Marion agreed to marry him, to ask if Dodger could start coming inside.

And she let him stay inside for the whole night. Whilst Puddle's was meowing and scratching at the kitchen door, Graham distracted Marion by giving her multiple orgasms for the rest of the evening.

The following morning, Marion rushed out of the door, late for her meeting at work. Graham had the day off, and spent most of the morning in bed with Dodger. He would have to wash the bedding, he thought, because having the dog inside was one thing, but having him on Marion's bed was another.

As Graham stripped the bedding and walked down the

stairs, Dodger followed behind him, wagging his tail and squealing. "Alright, boy, don't worry. I'm getting you breakfast in a minute."

With the bedding in one arm, Graham opened the laundry room door. "Shit!" He dropped the bedding. "Puddles!" The cat darted from the room. "Dodger, Dodger, no, no!" But it was too late. The cat and dog rolled around the kitchen floor, growling, hissing and squealing, until all that was left of Puddles was a matted heap of black, bloody fur on the floor.

"Dodger!" Graham roared. "What have you done?"

Marion

The first thing she noticed when she arrived home that evening, was the house. It was sparkling. Secondly was the smell of roast chicken. Marion smiled and revelled in the fact she'd not only picked up a handsome man, but one that could clean and cook in her absence.

On the dining table was a bottle of champagne, and a bunch of red roses. Graham was standing over the stove, sweat dripping off his forehead.

"What's the occasion?" Marion asked, dumping her bag on the kitchen counter.

"We did get engaged last night, didn't we?"

Marion laughed and sat down at the dining table, and, when Graham wasn't looking, poked her tongue out at Dodger, who was squealing at the back door. She'd be dammed if he was going to get any leftover chicken, that was all for Puddles.

"How was your day?"

"Good, great," Graham said.

A few minutes of sipping champagne later, and Graham popped a plate of the most delicious- looking food in front of her. Grilled chicken, roasted veg and mashed potatoes with a creamy sauce. The buttery smell of the potato made her salivate.

"Just nipping to the toilet, love," Graham said, and Marion tucked into her food.

Once they'd finished eating, Graham spent an hour massaging her feet. She'd wondered what she'd done today that had made him so attentive. It was getting late, though, and she really did need to feed Puddles. Getting off the sofa, feeling pampered and appreciated, she called for Puddles. "Come on kitty, dinner time." She shook the pouch of food. That's strange, she thought. Puddles always comes running in at the sound of the foil packet. "Chu chu chu, come on, puss puss."

"Puddles," Graham called. "Dinner time, boy!"

Marion was unable to concentrate over the barking of Dodger at the back door. "Not you, you stupid dog!"

"Hey, hey, now, there's no need for that."

Marion shook her head. "Sorry, I just, this isn't like Puddles."

"He'll be around here somewhere. Come on, we'll look together."

Graham

He hated lying to Marion, but he knew if he told her the truth, it would be the end of their relationship, and he didn't want that. So, when he said he was going to the toilet before dinner, he snuck off and opened the front door.

"I've never left the front door open before, I-I-" Marion fell into Graham's arms.

"There, there, love. You've had a stressful day at work and you just weren't thinking. I'm sure he can't have gone far."

Graham agreed to drive around looking for Puddles.

He also agreed to print off some missing posters. After two hours of sticking posters to trees, lampposts, and through letter boxes, it was past midnight when they arrived home. He spent the night cuddling Marion, feeling quite happy Dodger had killed the little rat.

Marion

She phoned in sick the following morning, and stayed by the phone for the entire day. Tracie had come round to say, 'sorry to hear about Puddles,' but Marion didn't want to see anyone that day. She'd never been so devastated in her life. Her eyes, jaw and stomach were all aching from the tears she had cried. The phone rang, and Marion answered immediately. "Hello?"

"Any news?" Graham asked.

"No, none. Will you please stop ringing? Someone might be trying to get through." She hung up, and continued to wait, when she had the most reassuring thought she'd had all day. The cameras. She'd had a security system installed through her whole house when she'd suspected her husband was cheating on her. That's how she discovered her husband shagging his secretary in the kitchen, the laundry room, the bedroom, the bathroom, and just about everywhere. The cameras were so inconspicuous, tiny little things hidden in each corner of the room.

She jumped to her feet and rushed into the study. She clicked on the log that held the recording from yesterday. Sitting back in her chair, her cheeks burned as she watched herself having sex with Graham. She quickly fast forwarded through the night, thinking how sweet it was that Graham had held her right through until the morning. She let the recording play in real time the moment she saw Dodger on the bed.

She couldn't believe it. Graham having that dog on the bed was worse than seeing her ex-husband shagging another woman on the bed. Her blood boiled. Graham would get a right mouthful when he arrived home from work.

She continued to watch Graham taking the bedding off, then switched camera views, watching him walk into the kitchen. She decided she shouldn't be mad at Graham, after all, he did pamper her for the entire night, and she'd never known a man wash the bedding before.

Her heart exploded when she spotted Puddles running out of the laundry room, straight into the mouth of Dodger.

"Oh, oh, lord, no. No, Puddles, my poor Puddles," she cried, hands cupped over her mouth as she watched Graham shouting and holding his hands to his head.

You bastard, she thought. How could he instil false hope in her, going along with her to pin posters up and look for Puddles, when he knew her cat was dead the whole time? Bastard!

She continued to watch, eyes wide, heart still racing as Graham picked up Puddles and flung his body into a plastic bag. Then he spent some time scrubbing the floor, and disposing of any evidence.

She spent the next hour throwing up.

Tracie

She couldn't believe it. And she wasn't surprised that Marion had spent so long throwing up. Poor Puddles. As much as she thought Marion's obsession with Puddles was unhealthy, she never would have wished the cat any harm.

Tracie was worried for her friend, more now than ever. Her eyes were bloodshot, her brown hair was a mess, and her hands were visibly shaking on her lap. Marion noticed the engagement ring had also been removed.

"I'm going to kill him."

"Who?"

"I'm going to kill Dodger, right in front of Graham. Heck, I might even kill Graham."

Tracie shook her head. "Don't talk so daft, Marion. What you need to do is call the police." She stared at Marion as she rose to her feet. "Do you want me to call them?"

"No…I'll do it. I'll phone the police."

Graham

After a busy day, Graham was looking forward to coming home to a cooked meal. He was almost disappointed there was nothing left of Puddles. Cat meat was by far the best meat he'd ever tasted. "Mazzy, I'm home."

He took his jacket off and strutted into the living room. Marion was sitting on the sofa, with a bottle of vodka in her hand. "Mazzy?"

"Hello, Dear. Have a nice day, did you?"

"Err, yeah. It was okay. Are you drunk?"

"I've had a change of heart," she slurred, getting to her feet. "I think we should let Dodger inside, for good."

Graham smiled. "You sure?"

"Positive, darling. What, with Puddles being gone, we need another pet to take his place, don't we? Go on, go and let him in."

Letting the dog inside, Graham ruffled Dodger's head, giving him a good scratch behind the ears. "Allo, mate. Did you miss your daddy? Yes, you did!"

Marion came charging with a shovel in her hands,

screaming at the top of her lungs. She whacked Dodger on the spine with the shovel. The dog squealed and scattered away, Marion chasing after him like a mad woman. Just as she was about to smash Dodger over the head, Graham jumped in front. "Marion!" he yelled. And the shovel crashed into Graham's skull.

Marion

She didn't stop. Even when Graham was on the floor, she continued to scream, her blood on fire, fuelled by hatred, smashing his head until he no longer made a sound, or a movement.

Breathing heavily, she dropped the shovel to the ground and stared at him. It wasn't pretty. "You bastard," she cried.

She heard a growl. A vicious growl.

Her already racing heart nearly ran out of her chest as she turned to face Dodger, all teeth on show, snout wrinkled and drool dribbling to the floor.

Tracie

She heard Marion screaming, and jumped to her feet. All she could think of was Marion's words today – that she was going to kill the dog, and possibly Graham. Tracie hadn't thought much of it, but now, she feared the worst.

She reached the front door, and the screams became louder. Then she heard something else. It sounded like a grizzly bear. Tracie's heart palpitated at the sound. She flung the front door open and popped her head outside. Marion was on the front lawn, screaming as the Rottweiler mauled at her face.

"Marion!" Tracie screamed, her legs going weak as she ran toward her friend. Someone from across the street opened their front door, and Tracie yelled at the lady to phone the police and an ambulance. She continued to scream at the dog. "Get off of her! Stop. Oh, my god! Someone help!" Even in her adrenaline rushed state, Tracie couldn't find the bravery to try and pull the dog away. She feared for her own life.

When the dog finally stopped, it scurried inside with its tail between its legs, and Tracie ran over to Marion, but she was dead. Her face was unrecognisable. Tracie turned around and threw up there and then. From inside the house, she could hear the dog howling, almost painfully.

Minutes passed, and Tracie stood on the curb outside of Marion's house, along with a few other neighbours from the street, who were all already conspiring about what could have happened.

Eventually, an ambulance showed up, along with a patrol car. Tracie watched in dismay as her friend's body was taken away. She spent the next hour or so talking to an officer, and she was shocked to find out that Graham was inside, dead. Tracie couldn't answer the officer when he asked her if she had any idea what had happened that evening. She explained that she heard some commotion, but didn't think much of it as it was a regular occurrence from Marion. She didn't want to admit that Marion could well have killed Graham in a fit of anger. She didn't want people around here remembering her friend as a murderer.

She showed the officer to the front door.

"If you think of anything else, give me a call." He handed her a card.

Tracie nodded and sniffled. "I will…wait…what will happen to the dog?"

"He'll be put to sleep."

Tracie closed the door, hardly able to process the night's events. A missing cat. Two dead bodies. And a dog about to be put to sleep. How did something that looked so promising turn out such a tragedy?

**Five months later
Tracie**

Tracie still hadn't gotten over what had happened to Marion. She sometimes dreamed of her, mostly of the state her face was in. A local journalist wrote an article claiming the deaths had been caused by a lovers' tiff, a romance gone bad, possibly because of Graham cheating. But Tracie knew differently. Even though she never thought of Marion as a person to hurt a fly, let alone a human, she knew what had happened that night. Marion had snapped and killed Graham, in vengeance for Puddles. And in vengeance for Graham, Dodger killed Marion. It was an obsession, and a love for their pets that had killed them.

She couldn't help but blame on herself, even though at the time, she thought Marion's threats were all talk. If she had said something, rang the police and told them what Graham had done, and that Marion was threatening to kill him, this could have been prevented.

She peeped through the window at her new neighbours, who were carrying cardboard boxes from a removal van. She'd been wondering for a few weeks who her new neighbours would be after a sold sign was placed out front. Putting on her best smile, Tracie stepped outside and decided to introduce herself to the young couple.

"Hi, I'm Tracie. I live next door. Just thought I'd come say hello and welcome you to the neighbourhood."

"Oh, thank you. I'm Tabby, this is my boyfriend,

Luke."

The tall, blond, strapping young lad extended his hand and Tracie gave it a brief shake. "Well, let me know if you need anything. It's a nice neighbourhood, everyone is very friendly."

"Thank you," Tabby said. "We couldn't believe how cheap the place was. We've been looking at this part of town for months. Everything else was so expensive."

Tracie bowed her head slightly, wondering if she should tell Tabby that the house was probably so cheap because two people, a cat, and a dog perished there, but thought better of it.

"Actually," Luke said. "If you're not busy now, we could really do with a hand getting some of this furniture in. Tabby has a bad back."

"Yes, of course." Just then, another van pulled up.

"Oh, they're here!" Tabby said with a ridiculous amount of excitement.

"Oh, do you have children?"

Tabby shook her head and grabbed hold of Tracie's hand, pulling her toward the van. How nice, Tracie thought, to have such a nice, young couple move in. Tracie had never had a daughter, and thought Tabby fit the bill perfectly. Someone she could fuss over.

Dropping Tracie's hand, Tabby opened the back of the van.

Tracie took a step back. There, in the back of the van, were two cages. One with a black and white cat. The other with a brown Pitbull. "This is my cat, Trixie, and this is Luke's dog, Benji."

As Tracie watched Trixie hiss at Benjie, and Benjie growl in return, she placed a hand to her forehead, suddenly feeling the ground falling beneath her feet.

Your World And Its Weather

W.D. Frank

We were always the only ones who could hold each other together.
Yet, it has changed.
Your world and its weather.
Every day I spend watching you lie and kill.
All because I could never cut our tether.
I brought you into this life of mine and I can't take you out.
I always used to lean on the shoulders of your innocence.
Yet, it has changed.
Your world and its weather.

I hate myself for what I have turned you into.
I never wanted this life to be yours, but I needed you.
I am so sorry for enveloping you in my warped world...
even if you have grown to like the view.
Yet, I suppose this sickness of ours was always meant to bloom.
Following crimson footprints, I have brought you to your doom.

I never thought I would see you like this.
Beating a cripple to death with your fists.
Yet, I needed what I never wanted.
My tormentor is laughing in the distance and I suppose you are a joke of his.
Part of me wishes I could have let you die as a kid, but

this is what we have.
This is it.
Through this bleak world we will drift.
In the darkness, we kiss.
Yet, it has changed.
Your world and its weather.
The universe is empty.
We are all there is.

Buried Doll

Tina Rath

I have lain here since that midnight
A girl gave me her rival's name
And laid me in this little grave
Where all my days are now the same.

I, that was made to please a child
She made a mommet for her hate,
But hate has given hope to me
And I will watch and I will wait

And I shall see another spring
And I shall have a second birth
And she shall rue my blossoming
When I break - mandrake - from the earth.

Johnny on the Spot

Yvonne Marjot

"I wonder what he's like." Anna strips the bed in the spare room, throwing the dirty sheets into the hallway before stuffing the pillows into new cases. Her sister's coming home for the weekend, and she's bringing the new man.

"What?"

Mum's in Anna's room, bunting her holiday case up into the top of the wardrobe, 'since I won't be needing it again this year,' although Anna knows she'll probably be fishing it out again before the month is up, if only for another weekend break.

"I said, I wonder what he's like. Have you met him at all?"

"No, Maisie's been very cagey. I thought she might tell me while we were up in Blackpool, but she never. You should have come, Anna. We had a laugh."

"No, thanks. I know what you two are like when you get together. I'd just cramp your style." Anna's like her Dad – happy in a historic house or a garden, and completely lost in the bright lights and bustle that her Mum and sister love so much. A weekend in Blackpool, complete with bingo and clubbing, is her idea of hell. *Each to their own*, she thinks as she wrestles with the duvet cover.

There's a faint squeak of brakes, and she twitches the net curtains aside to see a late model car drawn up to the kerb. She presses her nose to the glass as Maisie eases herself out from the passenger seat.

"He is quite a bit older than her," she says, as the man shuts his door and turns the key. "Handsome, though."

"Ooh, let's have a shufty." Mum pushes her aside and squints down towards the front gate. She puts a hand up to her mouth and moans as if in pain. "Oh my God, no."

"What is it?" Anna hardly gets the beginning of the question out before Mum flings herself out of the room and down the stairs. She's not in time to prevent Maisie opening the front door and ushering her intended into the lounge. Mum barges in, with Anna hot on her heels. "Johnny bloody Ross," she shouts. "What the hell are you doing in my house?"

Johnny aims his beaming face at Mum, and wraps a possessive arm around Maisie's shoulders, while the other gestures broadly at the room and its occupants. "Yeah, sorry about my little joke," he says. "I had a bit of trouble a few years back. Had to change my name and all that. But that's behind me now. I'm 'ere to make an honest woman o' Robbie's girl." The final sentence hints at northern roots under his cosmopolitan accent and Mediterranean veneer.

Maisie edges her way out from under Johnny's grip. She backs away from him, eyes on his face, and glances across at Mum, who is crying openly now.

"Johnny," Mum says. "Your own daughter."

"What?" A frown creases Johnny's boot-polish tan and he suddenly looks his age. "Naw. You're having a fuckin' laugh."

Maisie's face whitens. She puts one protective hand over the swelling below her rib cage.

"Naw, she's Robbie's wee girl. He was always sweet on you. Watching you. You probably had 'im right under my nose, I reckon, when them troubles came on me."

Mum makes her way to Maisie's side and the two women stare at the man with identical looks of horror on their faces. "You're a bloody fool, Johnny Ross," Mum says. "Rob was a virgin the day I married him."

Anna winces. This is one more piece of information she'd rather not know about her Dad. It's been said now, though. She can't unhear it. The blood drains from Johnny's face and he shakes his head.

"Jeez, Alice. Are ya sure?"

"Her name is Alicia." Johnny spins round and stares at Rob. "You never bothered to get her name right, you bastard. And now you've harmed another of my girls." He steps forward.

Johnny blusters, "I had no way o' knowin'. Look at 'em. Like as two peas in a pod. I fought she were your'n. It was a laugh, that's all. Having both your girls right under your nose."

The charming John Smith, whom Maisie had paraded before her parents in absentia, is no more. Johnny's roots are showing, and they're not pretty.

Anna slips out of the house and makes her way to Johnny's car. The street is quiet and empty; the rest of the nation has no idea that the bottom has just dropped out of Maisie's world. Anna slips the knife out of her pocket and unsheathes it. The blade gleams in the sunlight; she keeps it well sharpened – you never know when you might need to do a bit of awkward pruning.

She bends and inserts it into the tyre wall. It's an effort, but it slides home and she gives it a good wrench, before attending to the other tyres. She's not sure how long it will take for them all to go down, and it doesn't feel like nearly enough, but at least it's something. She tucks the knife away and lets herself back into the house.

The tableau in the sitting room is almost unchanged. Maisie looks as though she is about to collapse, and Mum is holding her up. Johnny's bluster has faded to a dull whine – even he can't quite think of a way out of this situation. Dad's face is grey, and he suddenly looks old. He eyes Johnny with utter contempt. "Get out of my house," he says.

Johnny rushes at Dad, who steps aside and holds the door open for him. As he passes, Rob puts out his foot and trips Johnny, who crashes headfirst into the wall on the other side of the hallway. Groaning, he pulls himself to his feet and lurches out of the front door, banging it behind him. A moment later, Anna hears the roar of the engine as the car pulls away, the tyres already squealing as they soften. Behind her, in the flowery comfort of her parents' front room, Maisie bends forward, grasping her belly, and begins to howl.

Anna steps out the front door and closes it gently. She can hear Maisie's anguish, repeating "Ah, ah, ah…" as if she has lost all her words, and Mum's sobs, and then, just as the door latches, the quiet, calm tones of her father. "There now, my lovely girls. There, now. Come on, then," as he gathers them in. She sits down on the doorstep and pulls out her knife. Carefully she cleans it, then begins to prune the climbing rose that sprawls over the trellis beside the door. It's all very well being ready to protect your family, but you might as well get a bit of gardening done while you wait.

Number Six

Charlotte Stirling

She was adorable. Long, smooth hair as timeless as black orchids and that 'hopeful yet submissive' cast in her eyes that he found so compelling. Yuki's skin was flawless – creamy and languid, so perfect for bruising and marks. Jonathan Rigby, a false name for a false man, felt content. Each year on his birthday he ordered something special, and Yuki promised to be the most perfect present yet.

The Japanese girl reminded him of Number Six a little. Jonathan had considered the pros and cons of twins or a double gift numerous times, but it always came down to what he could control most easily because that was the key to his psyche. His control and their resistance.

The first time, the very first time, he had cruised Chinatown for a 'present' with the neon signs and blinking chopsticks testament to the chaos that lived in his head, his blood had surged with silver bursts of joy.

But he failed to find the pristine, almond beauties that he had envisioned; being accosted instead by skinny, lame horses with bad teeth and rotting souls. The first one was literally torn apart. His rage and disappointment punching her body until there was very little 'girl' left – just a battered pumpkin head attached to a bloody, bowling pin. But the buzz, man, the buzz made him feel omnipotent. And like all addictions he had to feed it constantly.

****

Yuki had fulfilled her potential to perfection. And now, she sat silently on her knees, holding, as he had ordered her to, a pitcher of icy and unforgiving martinis. Jonathan sipped elegantly at the drink in his left hand. The other resting lightly around the back of the girl's neck. And Jonathan, once again, congratulated himself on his intelligence and superiority coughing slightly as a tickle bothered his throat. Women were so 'bovine' when push came to shove and he chuckled at his own macabre joke.

And the chuckle turned into a full-blown hack and, as his nervous system betrayed him, the glass fall to the ash wood floor and lay cracked like a plundered Shrikes' egg, as he tried to loosen the tightness about his neck.

His lungs began to constrict and paralyse and Jonathan Rigby, a false name for a false man, fell to his knees, urine dampening his trousers to mid thigh.

So engrossed with dying was Rigby that he failed to notice Yuki's tiny smile as she remembered her sister, Number Six, and all that had been done to her by the 'shiroi akuma' before her and how trusting Monsters can be in the twilight of their lust and arrogance.

Deleting Jessy

Angelika Rust

He really should finally delete her. Hell, it had been a year. It wasn't like Jessy was going to come back. There would never again be a little green dot next to her profile pic, telling him she was online and ready to chat the night away.

The cursor hovered over his friends' list. Her pic always came up first. Weird, that.

Christmas had been bad. He'd invited everybody to a bit of ditch-your-parents-and-get-pissed, and of course stupid Facebook had suggested he invite her. He'd got so drunk that night, Roger and Emily had to carry him home. His mom had thrown a fit. Like it was his fault the barman hadn't given a flying fuck about whether or not serving minors might be a good idea.

Her birthday had been worse. Logging in that day, getting notified he should congratulate her...it had been like a message from beyond.

He clicked on her profile. It was flooded with posts along the lines of 'Happy birthday, Jessy, wherever you've gone. Wish you were still here. Miss you so much.' He'd read them all, but never added any of his own. Somehow, it had felt wrong. Intruding. Like he'd be sending a message to some world he didn't know the rules of. Not that he understood the rules of this one.

Her own last status was pinned to the top. That, too, was weird. He'd never managed to pin a post. In groups, yes. But never on his wall. He was convinced it was actually impossible, but there it was, for the world to see.

Um, folks? Anyone awake and driving? I kinda got lost... *embarrassed face* Someone come pick me up?

Well, someone had come. He wiped at his eyes. Her father had called him the next day. He'd heard her mother wailing in the background. And those pictures on the news. Scarlet snow and a single tennis shoe.

A chat window popped up, startling him. The miniature version of Emily's sweet face grinned at him. She changed her profile pic at least once a week, but she was always smiling that joyful, infectious smile. Dimples, freckles, and strawberry ponytail, she was like a breath of country air.

Hiya, Jake xx You okay?

His gaze wandered over to all those minuscule faces at the right side of the screen. Jessy topped the list, like she always did. 365d, it said next to her pic. Three-hundred and sixty-five days since she'd last been online. One year.

Of course Emily would be the one to remember, and check to see whether he was all right. She'd been a good friend throughout the entire year, always there for him, always cheerful and encouraging.

Really pretty, too, and in a sweet, self-effacing way. Not like Jessy at all. That girl had always known exactly how many heads she could turn just by walking by. Strong, proud, and so damn hot. Emily...he smiled to himself, remembering the many times she'd rolled her eyes over Jessy's diva act. How she'd always been the one he called when Jessy had gone and broken his heart, over and over again. How she'd listened, that cute frown wrinkling her freckled nose, like she was seriously trying to think up a possible solution for his troubled love life, when all he needed was someone to vent to.

He shook his head, remembering the feeling of Emily's hand in his when she'd told him she'd always be there for him, long after Jessy was nothing but a rotting corpse in a cold, hard grave. He'd laughed then, and held up his hand for a pinky promise.

A week later, Jessy had been dead. Emily had kept her promise, like the good friend she was.

Yeah, she was different. Jessy had hung on to him like a spoiled kid to a toy. Constantly dropping him and trampling all over him, but too selfish to let someone else have him. Emily...Emily seemed to genuinely care.

His gaze came to rest on her pic again; the curve of her mouth, the dimple where her lips met her cheeks.

One small step, one minor act of courage, and she might be more than just a good friend.

Maybe it was time to move on.

I'm cool, he replied. *You free tomorrow?*
Yeah, she instantly typed back. *See a movie?*
Sounds good. Pick you up at seven?
Awesome xx

He leaned back, nodding to himself. Yeah, it was definitely time to move on. He clicked on Jessy's pic. Another chat window popped up.

With Jessy's face on. He stared at it in confusion until he realized what had happened. How dumb. He'd gone and opened a chat window to his dead girlfriend.

Spooky, that you could still do that, even if the person was six feet under.

A crazy notion struck him. For a moment, he hesitated, but then he leaned forward again, fingers on the keyboard.

Hiya. I guess we're through. I mean, you and I, he typed before he really registered what he was doing. He jerked and shook his head, then deleted it all again without hitting the enter key.

"Whatever," he said out loud, staring at her beautiful face, that luscious black hair, those deep, dark eyes. "I love you. Always will. But...it's time. I'm deleting you,

Jessy."

A tiny green dot appeared.

Oh no, you don't.

He pushed his chair backwards with a muffled scream. "What?"

I said you don't.

"This is a joke, right? Who is this? Roger?"

It's me, my love.

He heard a sound from below, like the door smashing open.

"Roger, this isn't funny."

I'm not Roger. I'm Jessy. Your one, true love. No one shall ever have you but me.

Footsteps now, heavy and dragging, creaked up the wooden stairs.

He jumped to his feet. "Fuck. Who is this? How can you even know what I'm saying? Is it the webcam? Am I on video? Shit!"

Only now did he realize that he was no longer alone in the house, and whoever was coming up, they certainly didn't sound like his mom wanting to check whether he was already in bed. He looked around frantically. Why didn't he play baseball? No bat, what else did he have?

The door burst open. Framed by the light from the hallway stood...something. Something humanoid. Long, dark hair surrounded a face half rotted away. Teeth shone through gray, translucent cheeks. A maggot was crawling from one eye.

"Hi Jake," the creature purred in Jessy's husky voice.

He issued a whimper, picked up his chair and hurled it.

She dodged it easily, laughing a rich, throaty laugh, just as a crash sounded from behind Jake. He threw himself to the ground as splinters and shards exploded in every direction. Someone landed on his back, he heard a guttural cry and a chop, thump, thump.

Squinting through his fingers, he looked up. Emily stood before him, panting slightly, a sword in her hand.

"That bitch, really," she sighed. "Super possessive, huh? Did you know she messaged me every single day since her death? Always, keep your hands off Jake, don't dare touch him, he's mine, you've done enough harm as it is, nag, nag, nag. If I had known that's how she'd turn out, I'd have cut off her head back then and buried it at a crossroads, then we wouldn't have had to deal with a freaking zombie right now."

"W..what d..do you mean," he stuttered, "back then? Did...I mean...was it you who killed her?"

Emily stooped to wipe her blade clean on the tattered remains of Jessy's funeral attire. Reaching out, she picked up the rotten head, which had rolled a few feet after she'd separated it from the neck, then stood back up, wiping strawberry strands off her face. Splattered droplets of gooey flesh smeared under her hand, adding gray streaks to the brown freckles on her fresh, innocent face. She giggled. "What, do I look like a killer to you? Anyway, gotta go. Need to get this buried before she gets any more funny ideas." She shrugged with a comical expression, lifting the head up by the hair. "The rest of her is a bit too heavy for me. Just get it buried in the garden, will you?"

She bent down again, and placed a kiss on his lips that whispered promises; then, carefully avoiding the serrated edges of the pane, climbed onto the window sill and out. Her voice chirped up one more time. "See you tomorrow!"

Burn

Ken Alexopoulos

Every last second remains burned into my soul, a chronological scar that stretches outward into an eternity. An open wound that stings from our combined sweat and sweetened by the caress of soft moans and violent whispers.

When we ended, you had asked me if I meant what I had said. I promised the vast expanse of a thousand seas, or the threat of a crushing defeat that could annihilate my heart wouldn't stop me from fighting to reach you. I did. It was sworn as easily as I might take a breath.

You questioned your worth and wondered if the pain was justified or just a passing dream. I refused to accept the possibility. You were the definition of everything I could have wanted out of life, a fragile and perfect mess that embodied beauty and potential, the storm that lay just over the horizon.

I lay in that bed of lies and passion, pressed against the small of your back as I held you tighter, wanting to melt into your body. The one regret I have is that it was never possible to sink into your flesh.

In the end, when the sun began to rise and I had to take my leave to protect your virtue, one which remained unsullied and pure despite broken vows and heated infidelity against a man who couldn't understand you in the slightest, I told you that I would keep you safe from harm. Even if I might be the cause of what made you hurt.

I told you that if you were happy, I would vanish.

You asked if I would ever truly know if you were happy. That you could fake sincerity with a smile and the truth would be elusive.

I know you.

I have known you.

I could pick your face from a crowd of millions.

I would be able to hear your voice from across the planet.

I could see your smile from behind a mask and see your tears in ocean waters.

The problem is, I'm too damn noble to let you know any of that.

So I'll wait.

Until the world ends.

Valentine's Day

T.M. Hogan

My husband doesn't believe in Valentine's Day. "It's just a gimmick to make people blow money, just like Mother's Day, Easter, and Christmas," he says, so we never celebrate it. He also doesn't remember anniversaries or birthdays and never makes an effort to buy me gifts or act enthusiastic about doing something for me. In our eleven-year relationship together, I've received a gift once on Valentine's Day. Once! It was a bouquet of tiger roses, when I was seventeen and knocked up.

Nine years after that gift, and a week before Valentine's Day, this is how the discussion went:

Chris comes into the bedroom and suggests we have a date night when he returns from Melbourne. He'll be away for three days with the guys for a buck's party whilst I'm home alone taking care of the house and our three young children.
I sit up in bed, pulling the blankets around my body. "I was thinking we'd wait until Deadpool comes out and go for dinner and movies then," I say to him. "It's going to be Valentine's Day weekend."
Chris smirks with a guilty look in his eyes, "Oh, Stacey. I didn't think you liked... were into... Deadpool."
I look at him dumbfounded and about to start crying again. I just got over crying about him not wanting to

cuddle after making love. "I've been talking to you about this for the past two years and telling you how I can't wait to see this when it comes out. Not the mention all the Deadpool shit I've been sharing on Facebook lately, and you don't know I'm into it?"

"It's not confirmed yet," he says lightly, trying to keep me happy and calm.

"Oh, so there's an event, another event, that I'm not invited to," I say angrily. He knows how lonely and left out I feel.

"No, babe, its fine," he says, as I bury my face into my hands and silently sob. He sits on the bed near my feet and tries to explain himself. "It's Jamie, you know how he's shit at planning stuff. He says throw a LAN party, so I do, and he doesn't even show up," Chris adds, as if this is to comfort me.

"You are such a piece of shit," I say, staring deadly at him. My face wet with tears. "You never remember anything I say to you." He smiles at this, guilty as charged.

"You plan it, ok," he says, standing up to leave, "let me know when, and I'll tell Jamie," and walks out the room. Back to his games and the boys online waiting for him.

Ten minutes later, I've been able to sort out a group date to see Deadpool. God knows why Jamie is determined to have a get together on Valentine's Day – I thought I was meant to be organising this. He doesn't have a girlfriend or a date, and all the men are working that day. Thursday 11th would have been preferable because they are all rostered off work. This means no dinner before or after the film.

Five tickets for Sunday 14th February for me, Chris, Jamie, Ivan and his partner Stephanie. You know what? Maybe I should just pretend Jamie is my boyfriend for the night! Better yet, I'll steal Stephanie and make out with her in the back seats of the cinema.

Sex in Santo Domingo

Bradley Darewood

Most of this anthology is fiction, but given my uncanny ineptitude with everything from relationships to sex, I thought an excerpt from my memoir in progress might be in order. The story is true, but it goes without saying that I've changed the names, and the timeline is compressed for coherency.

It was the turn of the millennium when I first moved to the 500-year-old metropolis of Quito, nestled high above the clouds in the Andes mountains.

The Plaza de Santo Domingo was a special place. Stone colonial buildings loomed above the cobblestones in Quito's historic center. The trolley's bell was inaudible in the throngs that populated the plaza by day. For one dollar a night, the hotel Reina de Cisne was my home.

The kind people of the day escaped with haste as soon as the sun set; by night the plaza was hollow. Dark figures loomed in the shadowy crevices where buildings met. And the archway… "Don't go that way. Ever. Don't ever go that way," my friend Ruso told me. Now and then a distant cry would waft through that narrow street, a corridor with no escape.

At night, I would throw my hood up when I left the trolley, and cross the plaza as fast as I could--slow enough not to cause suspicion, but fast enough to evade capture by the approaching shadows.

When I reached the warm light of the Reina de Cisne, I always breathed a sigh of relief, and took my seat next to Ruso and his sawed-off shotgun. His imposing figure guarded a table where the patrons sat, chatting amicably. Prostitutes, drug-dealers and beggars. And others, whose professions were… unclear.

My friend Domingo had come to the chilly urban capital of Quito in search of money. He was originally from rural Manabi, Ecuador's coastal countryside, but there was little money for beggars in the remote parts of the hills. He had been run over by a train as a child, his right leg severed at the knee, and manual labor was scarce in Manabi. This is not to say he wasn't strong – Dom was incredibly fit. With the prosthetic leg he attached to his knee he ran, played sports, did handsprings, and backflips. To be honest, he was jacked. I wished I had half of his muscles.

Dom sold candies on the bus. He would hide his false leg in his room, and pull out polio crutches (normal crutches didn't have as crippling of an effect), then board the bus by the park. "Ladies and Gentlemen!" he would announce as he stumbled down the walkway, passing out plastic-covered homemade chocolates. "These are traditional chocolates from the province of Manabi. I am a hard worker, but as you know life presents us all with many challenges. Please find it in your heart to support me with a small purchase of this delicious chocolate."

Buses in Quito are like a social service agency of their own; a parade of people like Dom pass out candies, prayer cards, CDs, play music, all with a sad story. Thankfully, the people of Quito are generous. Infinitely kinder than the people of my homeland.

"I want to come to your country one day," Dom said to me as we sat outside the Reina de Cisne. "How much does someone make selling chocolates on a bus in the United States?"

"We don't… I mean we don't really do that."

"What do people do?"

"Work at McDonalds maybe."

"How much do you make at McDonalds?"

"Five dollars an hour."

"Five dollars?? I make eight dollars in an hour!"

Dom lived across the hall from me. He shared a room (and a bed) with his best friend from Manabi… and his friend's girlfriend. The girlfriend was a recent addition, a thick prostitute, bursting out of her torn fishnets. The three lay snuggled together when I visited his room, filling the entirety of a bed made for two.

"This is Teresa," Dom introduced me from the edge of the bed.

"I *love* gringo dick!" she said, licking her fingers before offering her hand for me to shake.

"Uh, thanks," I took her hand awkwardly. It was still wet.

Dom got off the bed and walked me into the hallway.

"Can I... stay in your room tonight? I think my friend wants some time alone with Teresa."

Getting ready for bed, Dom looked at me quizzically as I put on sweatpants and jumped in bed next to him.

After a pause, he said, "You're not going to take off your pants?"

"Um... no. It's really cold in Quito."

Dom wasn't the first guy to ask me to take off my pants that week. Yesterday, one of the other patrons of the Reina de Cisne had been sitting with his girlfriend at the table outside, staring steamily at my crotch. "My girlfriend really wants to try gringo cock," the guy said, licking his lips while he stared at my package. "Do you want to come upstairs?" In the last month I'd been asked by guys to share a prostitute seven times, to take off my pants three times, and one guy decided not to bother with pretense at all and straight out asked if he could see my dick. I was twenty-one years old, but sex was still an enigma for me, and the whole thing left me puzzled. Given the sheer frequency that guys wanted to see my penis, I wasn't sure it was entirely sexual.

"Why do guys in Quito always want to see my dick?" I asked Dom as we lie back to back in bed.

"Well," he paused, pondering. "All of the porn here is made in the United States. It's all white people. And they all have huge dicks. People are probably just curious."

I decided to give Dom a little space to sleep and walked to the entryway of the hotel. The night staff, Raul, sat there watching television from a seat in the lobby. He had a leather jacket with a Tweety Bird patch sewn onto the breast. A Tweety Bird tattoo adorned his left calf as well.

"Hello Bradley," Raul said with a smile.

"Hi Raul."

"It's late."

"Yes, it is."

"We should get a prostitute."

I can't count the number of times I'd been invited to get a prostitute. Sex for money is an ethical conundrum for me. While I acknowledge that prostitutes need the money, I could never really bring myself to sleep with someone who had to be paid to do it. It just feels exploitative. That explanation was lost on Ecuadorian men of the Plaza de Santo Domingo, where sex with prostitutes was something of a weekly sport. No one seemed to believe the truth, so lies were the easiest way to refuse.

"I really can't, Raul. I'm worried about diseases."

Raul nodded thoughtfully. "Well, how about a donkey then?"

I didn't know what to say.

"My cousin has a donkey," Raul continued, his voice silky with desire. "Donkey pussy is soooo tight. And you don't even need to wear a condom!"

"I-- uh-- where I'm from-- we-- uh… don't do that."

I made my way back to my room. Dom was still awake. I lay in bed next to Dom staring at the ceiling, not sure what to make of the offer I had just received.

"Dom?"

"Yeah?"

"I just got invited to fuck a donkey. Is that normal?"

Dom paused. "Ummmm…. no…"

There was something to that pause. I turned to look at him. "Wait, have *you* had sex with a donkey?"

"No…." his eyes wandered as the word trailed off unconvincingly.

"You have!"

"Well… maybe."

"What do you mean maybe? Is it normal to have sex with donkeys here?"

"Well, my grandmother has a farm…"

Dom had been very horny as a child. He'd had sex with the dog, the cat, chickens.

"Wouldn't the chicken scratch you?"

"Not if you hold its feet. But I only did it once."

Apparently, fucking a chicken kills it. It had been hard to explain to the family, and no one would eat it afterwards. He seemed ashamed, recounting his exploits until he got to the last of the farm animals.

"Yes, I had sex with the donkeys, but I also had sex with… Chalina…" His eyes got steamy when he said the name and he shifted his crotch.

"What's a Chalina?"

"Chalina is the name of my grandmother's horse."

"Isn't it dangerous to have sex with a horse? I mean, it could buck you and kill you or something."

"You have to ask it first!"

"Ask it?"

"Yes! You stroke its mane like this," he waved his hand in the air simulating the gentle way he ran his fingers through Chalina's hair, "then whisper in her ear." He moved forward, his lips pursing seductively. "Do you want to have sex with me?"

"And how do you know the answer?"

"If she does this," Dom rolled his eyes with a warning grunt, "it means 'no'." Yes was a much more inviting grunt.

The next day, I decided to try and confirm my new knowledge of sex with horses. I hunted down a friend of mine who works with a sex education non-profit. His organization disseminates condoms to youths, and works on preventing teen pregnancies; I figured he'd be able to help me interpret the experience.

"In the cities, donkey sex isn't all that typical," he told me, "but the countryside is another story. Perhaps you have the same in your country?"

As a city kid, I'd never been invited to join in any donkey sex growing up… but there *are* countless cow-sex/cousin-sex jokes aimed at my rural trailer-dwelling relatives, and of course there's all the European jokes about goat-fucking farmers.

He continued, "Manabi is a special case."

"Why is that?"

"Male virginity."

Male virginity is a big deal in Ecuador. Pulling back the foreskin for the first time is something akin to breaking a man's hymen. In the province of Manabi, losing your virginity is necessary to become a man. It's a coming-of-age thing, expected to occur on a man's sixteenth birthday. Unfortunately, while promiscuity is celebrated among men, it's stigmatized among women. So in small towns there's a dearth of women with which to lose one's virginity. That's where the farm animals come in.

I took the bus back to the Plaza de Santo Domingo. A young girl, with pigtails and a hot pink backpack, took a seat across the aisle from me. I couldn't count the number of times she ogled me, then hastily brushed back her hair. It was making me uncomfortable. How old was she? Thirteen?

A look of determination on her face, she took a piece of paper out of her bright pink backpack with stars on it. She looked up at me once again, then wrote something. As she got up to leave for her stop, she slid the paper into the seat next to mine. On it was scrawled her name and number, complete with cutesy hearts. Even if she had been ten years older, it still would have been creepy.

I stared at the paper, disturbed, until I was interrupted by a chocolate in my lap. A traditional chocolate from Manabi.

"Bradley!" Dom said with a welcoming smile. He grabbed my hand with a lingering handshake. "You can keep the chocolate. I'll see you later."

Later was there before I knew it, with Dom staying in my room for another night. We lay in bed (with my pants firmly on) and talked. Reaching into my pocket, I took the paper with the cutesy hearts on it and tossed it into the small plastic trash bin across the room.

"What was that?" Dom asked.

"Just a phone number."

Dom frowned. "Bradley, can I ask you a personal question?"

"Sure." He'd told me about fucking a chicken. We were already on a personal level.

"Why aren't you married?"

I could have easily told him that I was too young, but

why was I single? I was essentially a virgin. Thoughts of donkeys and prostitutes swirled in my head. This week's candidates weren't exactly promising, but I couldn't help but be awe-struck by this strange thing we call sex: how varied it is, how easily I am disturbed by it. Perhaps, I mused, I'm disturbed by love as well. Disturbed because I'm afraid of it.

There was a certain free-spiritedness that Dom had that I didn't. The bravery to enjoy love and sex effortlessly. I didn't want to kill a chicken or exploit a prostitute, but admired Dom's ability to live life in a series of passionate encounters. It was an ability I didn't have.

Dom was waiting for his answer, but for some reason I just couldn't tell him all of those thoughts that whirled through my mind.

"I don't know," I lied.

Waiting

Chloe Hammond

So, is this how I will know?
Not a midnight phone call,
Or a cap-clutching police officer?
Instead, this slow waiting as you don't arrive,
Long seconds turning to hourly minutes
While the Reaper keeps company
Boney fingers grip my shoulder and strum
As we wait to see which of us
Can claim you.

Miss Angelika March

Charlotte Stirling

I never understood the appeal of Miss Angelika March. The charisma that the whole village seemed in awe of was lost on me. To deny her physical beauty would be petty, and a lie, but there was a taint to her like a broken drain whose slime and soil has seeped out to cover her skin.

The realisation that she had seduced my husband hit me quickly and slowly. A brutal wash boarding of truth that crackled about my ears and battered my trademark denial.

I saw them standing together, not touching yet, but so very together as if a slightly different light surrounded them. Not golden, but perhaps brass or pewter. Something common and easily led.

And then she touched his hand lightly and kept it there and I drew a breath to steady myself because when she looked at me, there was triumph riding high in her eyes. And I knew. And his hand then moved to cover hers and my husband of forty years saw me looking and didn't flinch. Just turned his face from me and I knew for a second time.

Then my heart turned hard and steel flooded those tight, little veins that feed the eye, and my mouth tasted the betrayal like an overnight locust storm.

This time, Miss Angelika March, there will be a comeback. Wait for it in the night when you take off your mask and your true nature reveals itself in the blacks and purples of deceit. I will smash that portrait in your attic and your world will be undone.

To Hell and Back

Jay Robbins

"Don't do anything crazy," she said, lying next to him in a room at the Sheraton.

"Of course," he replied.

It was winter and still dark outside, but graying as the last day in Wyoming began to rise with the members of the 2-300. Russell didn't generally spoon but made an exception for his last night with Alyssa. She deserved it. She was the best woman he could ask for, even if she had put on a little soft weight. He had even acclimated to it enough to genuinely be attracted to her pot belly and bigger thighs. The bigger cup size was nice too.

The most romantic gesture Alyssa could expect from her high school sweetheart was a pat on the ass when he opened the door for her. She always feigned anger but more often than not exposed a grin when catching his lusty gaze. She was wild for Russell and still stole glances at his Wrangler butt. She found any excuse to brag to her friends about his wiry yet strong build, earned roughnecking, cowboying, and hunting the Laramie Mountains. He had a body built for fucking, and never failed to please Alyssa in bed. With all portions of his life Russell took great pride in finishing a job well and quickly, and oddly applied that same pride to sex. Having them both reach climax in the first minute left so much more time for other pursuits.

Russell was not so good for lovemaking though, which made their last night together all the more special. He went slow, and kept her eyes wedded to his. He prolonged and delayed to stay inside her for as long as he could, once even stopping his stroke to make out with her until he knew he could keep going. They came together, and after remained entwined as one being for an hour or more, maybe for the last time.

"I'm not going to do anything stupid. I've got nothing to prove, Lys."

"Good. I need you, Russ. I need you to come home."

"I plan to. And I'm getting out. I don't need this fuckin' war. I ain't afraid. Just got better things to do than deal with a bunch of Arabs. I don't rightly care if Saddam runs the show or some other towel-head. All the same to me. Besides, folks should be puttin' Wyoming oil in their cars."

Alyssa seemed reassured. Russell never got hurt on the rig, nor riding rough stock. He was tough and smart in the way things worked in the world. The kind of smarts that can't be taught from a book.

"But there is one thing." There is always a 'but'. "They made me a sergeant. I didn't ask for it, but they forced it on me all the same. I have men that answer to me, just like on the rig, and their safety is my responsibility, just like on the rig. There is only one thing more important to me than coming home to you, and that's getting my boys home. I can't come back without them. Do you understand, Lys?"

"Yes, that's why I love you."

They married during Russell's two-week leave from Iraq, much to the chagrin of his brothers-in-arms, believing, generally correctly, that deployment marriages were doomed to fail. They said their vows below a waterfall, with few guests from either family being present, due to the cost of a near spontaneous trip to Hawaii. He chose to betroth Alyssa on this island paradise to make up for his very unromantic proposal, which essentially went, "Hey babe, we've been palling around for so long, what do ya reckon we go ahead and get married?" It was actually something Alyssa considered an endearing quality; she figured that if players were smooth talkers, then she had nothing to worry about with Russell.

They both thoroughly enjoyed their honeymoon at the Hale Koa resort on Oahu that catered to military personnel. Iraq wasn't discussed, but rather which sandal went with what dress. They dined on spam mushubees and chicken katsu curry, on freshly caught shrimp from off-the-radar shrimp shacks, and lobster tails in Pearl City. They ate and made love, both four or five times a day, Russell's desire for both being insatiable. Husband and wife were trying to create unlimited moments out of such limited time. Alyssa even got her new beau out to the beach. She couldn't help but laugh at the country boy with reddish-brown hands, neck, and face, contrasting hysterically with his wife-beater top and ghost white legs. Paradise could not last indefinitely, however, and soon Russell was back to the land of the two-way firing range. Before leaving, he made the promise young soldiers give to loyal brides: "One way or another, I will return to you." The honesty in his gaze brought some reassurance to his words.

Alyssa waitressed sixty hours a week at *Sanford's Grub and Pub* whenever extra shifts were available. She needed the money to make payments on the brand new double-wide she had signed the title on. She also had no need to spend a lot of time alone in a home shared by a husband residing on the other side of the world. She wore a yellow ribbon in her hair at work, and left a blue star banner in her picture window. She made a large framed photo collage of Russell and his soldierly exploits. She got involved in the local Family Readiness Group. She helped raise money to send locally-made beef jerky to FOB McHenry.

She wasn't quite prepared for the call that every Army spouse dreads. But she was thankful; her man was coming home and keeping his promise. Other families were not so lucky. She told Russell she would quit work and meet him at Ft. Lewis, to be with him during his rehabilitation. He told her to stay home, that it wouldn't be more than three or four weeks before he could get released to be with her permanently. When he arrived at Casper International Airport, Alyssa steeled herself to her husband's new appearance, hoping she wouldn't look shocked when she first laid eyes on him. She knew Russell had been sent home for a head injury, but she was too afraid to ask what that entailed for his face. She watched in nervous anticipation as her husband disembarked off the single engine plane. Fear turned to joy as her husband appeared before her whole, with no facial scars. She ran to him and hugged him tight, trying to wrap her arms around twice like *Stretch Armstrong*. His response was placid, subdued, and somewhat distant, giving her a kiss on the cheek and saying, "Let's go home."

Hawaii and Casper were two drastically different entities, and so was Russell, separated by a handful of months in that great chasm that swallows men whole. Now, he was camped out on a suede loveseat, only rising to change out the DVD in the player or to take another sip from his Vault, or chocolate milk, or blue raspberry slushy, all sitting in a row, ensconced in gas station food debris. Time of day had no meaning, any of three activities could occur at anytime, day or night. He was on his second Audie Murphy film for the current sitting, *Bad Boy,* having just finished *Red Badge of Courage.*

It took only a few weeks of refolding the guest blanket from the couch and picking up hot dog and *Tornado* wrappers and pop bottles from the living room floor for Alyssa to realize she was living with an imposter. She was sleeping with someone, but it wasn't the Russell that pampered her on an island paradise. His passion for her and for life itself was gone. They had sort of had sex once when returning home, but he couldn't look her in the eyes, and his mind wandered too much to finish. The doc at the VA gave him some *Citalopram* and dick pills, like being given an aspirin for a clogged emotional artery.

Since being back, Russell was tortured by the same nightmare.

His team is out on a routine mission on a flat, desolate highway, surrounded by endless beige-colored flakes of hardened, parched sand. His driver and gunner are in good spirits, chattering away with each other as if they were on I-25.

Ahead, Russell sees something ominous and foreboding. In the middle of the road sits a fallen angel, atop a throne of blood-encrusted Sapi plates and helmets, riddled with shrapnel shards, recesses filled with chunks of mandible, fragments of orbital, ulna, and tarsal bone, molars. Sun-bleached femurs, alternating with humeri, all sharpened to a point, jut out menacingly like rays from the back of the seat of death. The demon is cloaked in black goat skin; his elongated head, hooded by a freshly-skinned black panther replete with upper skull, revealing no face but infinite black, expanding forever inward. Russell is nearly catatonic with fear. He finds his voice when the many tails of the cloak expand outward, slithering and writhing across asphalt and sand; the tentacles dissipating at its ends into swirling ash and putrid smoke, pushing army debris, ammo can lids and MRE wrappers in its wake.

His growing terror thrusts air out of the lungs, forming a weak "Look," corresponding with a pathetic attempt to cover the scene with a spread-out hand on the windshield. His team does not notice the grisly figure, or his own wild gestures. They continue chattering with each other, and smiling, driving ever closer. Russell checks the switch on his Vic system, and waves over to his driver as he lets out a desperate scream. The call of warning is returned with apathy and a nod from the care-free figure behind the wheel, with the gunner swinging lazily back and forth on the turret's sling. Russell lets out a series of yelps, looking wantonly for any response, coming to the sickening conclusion that no sounds escape him. He drops his hand to look upon the agent of shadows, being too afraid to look away. His eyes track involuntarily into the dark spirit's obsidian eyes. The demon alone can hear his screams. Projecting out of the goat-skin sleeve, a rotting hand, palm skyward, dermis, muscle, and sinew sloughing off the telescoping metacarpals, slowly moves towards the body, confidently beckoning the truck toward an unseen oblivion.

Always just before his team is entangled in tentacled darkness, Russell would find the strength to peel his eyelids open to escape the oblivion overtaking him. He was thankful that his interactions with the demon did not awaken his exhausted wife. Nevertheless, falling asleep was a nightly fear, but drinking heavily before bed had a medicinal quality. It kept the dreams away.

An old high school friend (that hadn't joined up) had thought it would be nice to drop off a DVD for Russell in his mailbox. It was *Jarhead,* accompanied with a note that said, "Hey Bud, this movie was badass, thought you would like it." The thoughtful gesture was a mistake, as the friend would find out early one morning; he found the DVD case on his doorstep, inside was the disc, broken in half, accompanied by a rambling note.

```
Hey "Bud"
  There is nothin badass about some
dude acting hard and putting on a
uniform, making money looking like
Billy Badass while guys are slogging
around in the real shit downrange.
Then these fuckers become Wedding
Planners and gay cowboys and fairy
fuckin princesses their very next
movie. They're nothing but whores, and
they piss on the soldiering
profession. You know the pussy from
the Deer Hunter with De Niro?
  DON'T BE THAT GUY!
```

No, Russell stuck to Audie Murphy, because he wasn't an actor pretending to be a soldier, he was a soldier pretending to be an actor. Audie was Superman, dressed as Clark Kent to blend in with the mortals. Russell did more than watch, he observed, he studied. He didn't know how to act around people, in a way he preferred to be aloof from proper society, but love for his wife made him want to learn how to "act."

About three straight movies would be enough before Russell would take a drive in his tan '05 Chevy Silverado 2500 he had bought before the deployment to lock in the low interest rates guaranteed by law through the Soldiers and Sailors Civil Relief Act. He bought a Chevy because he came from Chevy people. At a Thanksgiving, years ago, Russell asked his grandfather how long their family had been comprised of Chevy men and he responded with, "Since we got off the fuckin' *Mayflower,* boy, since we got off the *Mayflower."*

On his daily trips, Russell might go rent half a dozen movies at Blockbuster; after all, he was fine with films that steered clear of the war genre. He would also end up at a convenience store or a supermarket to replenish his snacks and maybe grab a lunch. A few weeks after getting home, Alyssa sent Russell out for some shredded cheese. She was making his favorite, homemade tacos. She also offered to bake chocolate chip cookies but Russell declined, saying that since the incident, freshly-baked cookies just smelled burnt and as a consequence were inedible. So when he brought a big bag of shredded Monterey Jack to the register, he was appalled to find out that it cost ten dollars. He demanded a manager, who told him that the price was correct but that there were smaller bags that cost less. "No shit," was Russell's reply as he paid and walked out the door, vowing to himself that he would never be gouged by that store again.

    Now when he went out, he carried a fanny pack filled with ten dollars of loose change and a calculator. Some thrifty shoppers saved money by buying in bulk. Russell took the opposite route. He would make himself a sandwich at the store. A loaf of seven grain bread cost 2.13/14 slices = .15/slice x 2 slices = .30 cents. Then he went and took out a single slice of gourmet Monterrey Jack, leaving in the package 46 cents. The roast beef was harder, as it was packaged by the ounce. Russell had to put three slices of it in his hand and guess the weight. He judged the meat in his palm to be just under four ounces. He left behind 1.86 to err on the side of caution, sprinkling the change into the bag of roast beef before resealing it. He would then munch on his sandwich in full view of the condescending shift manager who had so angered him earlier. When the manager would look upon him in puzzlement, Russell would say, "Don't worry champ, your money is in the bag," while gesturing with his sandwich-filled fingers towards the bread aisle, before sauntering out. The manager would collect the loose change and add it to the store's incidental fund, throwing away the opened food and marking them down as spoiled. When employees would observe Russell's odd behavior, they would ask the manager what to do. The manager told them to leave the man alone, that based on his garb he must be a veteran, a victim of "that stupid war." His workers thought the manager was just a very thoughtful man, helping someone in need. The truth was much different. The manager had looked into Russell's dead eyes, and when Russell looked back, he looked *through* him, not at him. He also noticed that Russell had the habit of looking about the floor around the manager's feet. The manager was flat-out terrified of Russell; he knew it was in his best interest to let this sleeping dog lie. It was a good thing he did, for when Russell was scanning the cold floor around the manager's feet, he was visualizing where the dude would land after he got choke slammed, an anger management technique he learned in the Warrior Transition Battalion. Russell went off to war a collie; he came back an emotionally scarred pit bull. He wore the coin purse strapped to his waist everywhere, except for when he was with Alyssa. He wanted someone to say something, to laugh, but nobody ever did, not even at the bar.

Another destination on his trips away from the sofa was to Casper Mountain, or more specifically, the many switchbacks leading up to the top. Russell would make his way up the winding Casper Mountain Road. Once on top, he wouldn't get out to enjoy the outdoors or to look for solace others find in the wilderness. He would simply turn around and roll back down the same road to the base of the mountain. Each sharp U-turn, Russell would slow and look below for an oncoming car. If he was driving during the day, he would point at each passing vehicle with his index finger, dropping his thumb while whispering, "pop…pop…pop," the same thing he had done on the same road in the third row seat of his mom's yellow '81 *Suburban*.

At night Russell was afforded an opportunity to add some more realism to his ride on the switchbacks. He always had his .45 in the truck with him. In cover of darkness, he could drop the magazine and leave it on the passenger seat. Then he would push the ambidextrous thumb safety down and draw the stainless steel slide back, providing an escape for the round in the chamber. The loose cartridge he would keep in his mouth. He liked the taste of brass and carbon, flicking it and rolling it with his tongue over the bottom row of teeth, allowing the stray .45 ACP to rest behind his bottom lip, like a dip of long cut. Now, in the darkness, when confronted by oncoming headlights, he could pull on a real trigger, relishing the sound of the hammer striking against the base of the firing pin.

Russell considered these treks as a part of ongoing training. He was staying sharp, alert, striving towards rejoining his unit still downrange. He was also suppressing a new fear, forcing himself to drive towards a perceived threat while pulling the trigger. Once, on the steepest switchback, Russell wanted to see how fast he could go without flying off the edge. At the top of the bend, he revved the engine while in park, testing the 6 liter *Vortec 6000* V8 engine, bringing it up to 5000 rpms. Dropping it into drive, Russell steadily picked up speed, the automatic transmission changing smoothly into higher and higher gears. Two-thirds of the way down the truck got up to 68 MPH. When he reached the next-to-last reflector post, he slammed hard on the brakes, shimmying and skidding to an ignoble stop, the front end well off the black top. If he had stopped any later or gone any faster, he would have flown headlong off the precarious precipice on the outer edge of the unforgiving bend.

Alyssa was shocked their first night in bed when her

husband began to flail his arms wildly while jabbering incoherently. As if defending against ghosts or closet monsters she buried her head under the covers, feigning sleep, unwilling to let her husband know she was aware of his nightly visitor. One night while in R.E.M. sleep she caught a forearm to the forehead. Afterward she developed a nightly ritual: she would get in bed with her husband and wait for snoring, at which time she would move to a rocking chair and sleep under an afghan. At four A.M., she would get back in bed with her husband so he wouldn't wake up alone. Russell didn't notice his wife was not in bed upon awaking from his dream, because, out of shame, he would always shrug the blanket over his head and face the wall, hoping his unmanly shrieks had not awoken his bride.

Alyssa spent more time at work, thinking about how poorly she would be judged by her peers if she left a recently-returned, wounded combat veteran. She fought the words "separation" and "divorce" from overtaking her thoughts. Her family made it worse, as they saw their out-of-work son-in-law as lazy, milking the deployment and what they perceived as a bad headache. On bad days, when she had worked too late and her husband was on another excursion, she would allow herself to entertain the idea of leaving him. She would work out the logistics and how to broach the subject. And always, right before telling him, she would receive a heartfelt voice mail that would start out with: "Remember when we were making out along the creek bank at the state fair, and that guy tripped over us…", or a text that read: "Remember when we got lost in Waianai? Arn't you glad we are spending 'kill Haole day' in Casper, babe?" Russell's unique and laconic messages of love would reinvigorate Alyssa, giving her a fresh boost to double her efforts at salvaging their relationship. Whether it was making a special dinner or bringing home the Audie

Murphy Movie Pack, which she would soon regret, Alyssa wanted her man to know that she loved him, and was proud of his sacrifice.

With the passing weeks, she learned to limit the expectations she had for her husband as far as affections went. He was never able to express himself in person, only through notes and electronics. A major breakthrough occurred when she was able to rest her head on his lap or hold hands during one of the frequent movie nights, as long as she stuck to harmless small talk or didn't talk at all. Her heart fluttered like a virgin's when Russell actively placed his hand on her thigh one night on the loveseat. She had the urge to light candles and suggest they sit Indian-style and get lost in each other's eyes. She had an equal desire to guide his hand a little farther north. But she did neither, not wishing to push her luck, knowing that just because a wolf allows you to give him a scrap of meat, it doesn't mean he is ready to be petted. She simply rested her head on his sturdy shoulder, and allowed herself a little smile.

Things were not perfect, of course, but they seemed to be getting better. In two days, Bravo Battery would be landing in Casper from Ft Lewis, after finishing a grueling year-long stint in Northern Iraq. She hoped that the arrival of guys like Miller and Cabelo would provide an outlet that she couldn't. In any case she would be able to compare notes with the other wives' homecomings to see what was normal and what wasn't. She was so at ease and looking forward to the homecoming celebration at the airport that she fell asleep before Russell. She needed it, as she was filling in for someone's shift so she could take the next day off to see the rest of the boys come home. It proved to be a mistake, as she awoke from a beautiful dream with a stinging shot to her right eye. She had let her guard down by not moving to the rocker, and was rewarded with a swollen black eye.

When Russell awoke, he got to see his own handiwork, despite Alyssa's best efforts at covering it up. Tears welling in both their eyes, Russell asked sincerely, "Was that me?" Alyssa made a commendable attempt at convincing her husband that it was an honest mistake and not a big deal, but her eyes and trembling fingers betrayed the fear Alyssa had developed for her scarred husband. That look finished the job started in Iraq; it crushed him, mind and soul. Alyssa gave her man a deep kiss, of which Russell, for the first time since being home became an active participant. She then left promptly, under the auspice of being late for work.

Russell spent the rest of the morning watching videos from his honeymoon, and a little from the wedding, although he hated ceremonies. He watched them to see what his wife looked like happy, to use it as a reference point for how she looked now. He also watched to be reintroduced to the pre-blast Russell, the guy with dreams and a future, and a soul.

Recalling his wife's terrified expression that morning, Russell realized that she had known of the dreams all along, that she was also tortured by it. He knew that there was only one thing he could do. He left for his favorite grocery store and returned home with a single red rose, which meant some lucky lady in the near future would receive a watered vase with eleven roses, four quarters, a nickel, and four pennies. He went to the kitchen and peeled off a sheet from the magnetized shopping list pad with a cornucopia background. He jotted down a quick note and took off his ring. He rolled the note up and placed it within the ring, placing the stem of the rose within the note, placing the triad upon the tiled counter top. He made himself a glass of chocolate milk and watched *To Hell and Back*, hoping Audie could give him the courage for what had to be done. When the credits rolled, he left his wife's house and mounted his Chevrolet steed for a ride to the switchbacks.

It was dark when he reached the steepest stretch of switchback that he earlier conducted his training on. He let the truck idle in park at the upper end of the stretch while he sent a voice message off to his wife, knowing that she kept her phone on silent at work. That benign task thus completed, he moved on to the more malignant one. He dropped the safety and jacked a round into the chamber of his .45, then dropped the magazine. After all, he only needed one round and he didn't want some dipshit with the volunteer fire department to blow a toe off playing with a loaded weapon; safety first. With his sidearm ready, Russell punched the gas. By the time he reached the second to last reflective post before the bend he was going 75, a speed of no return. As he reached the edge of the precipice he pulled the trigger, which released the spring, swinging forward the hammer, thrusting forth the firing pin into the center fire primer, igniting the smokeless powder, propelling the spinning hollow point projectile into Russell's wounded brain, mercifully killing him as his truck flew off the edge, rolling hundreds of yards down the side of Casper Mountain. He faced his demon, driving headlong into its deathly throne, finding solitude on the other side.

Alyssa felt bad about doing a double shift and leaving her husband like that. So at 7:30 in the evening, she sat down at a table yet to be bused to check her messages. Seeing that there indeed was one, she typed in her code to listen.

"Alyssa, when a couple is stranded in the ocean, they face tough decisions. When fatigue and despair sets in, one of them might not be able to tread water. And as they begin to thrash around, they may start to drop under, and in a panic, they may hold on to the only thing there is in the whole ocean to hold to: Their loved one. They might begin to go down together, not because they had both lost the ability to survive, but because one is dragged down by the other, drowning both. In that case it would be a courageous act not to swim for shore, or to fashion a raft out of dead mackerel, but simply to let go. Alyssa, you are a strong woman, a good swimmer, and I love you too much to see you drown. I love you. Goodbye."

Alyssa raced to her car, terrified at what she might find, making it home in record time after bottoming out on gutters and speed bumps. She nearly battered down the door coming in to her spotless house. Red transplanted on white caught her eye as she grasped for the note, pulling it out of the ring and off the rose stem. Her eyes darted back and forth across the little sheet of paper. Her shaking fingers released the note as she slumped to the linoleum floor, beginning the mourning process in earnest.

The note read: "I've gone to look for Cougan, don't wait up."

Eternal Love

Bradley Darewood

Every time you touch me the world dissolves.
Your eyes locked in mine,
our bodies entwined
forever
…which was actually four months.
That clicking thing you do with your mouth?
Could you stop?
Oh god, did you just pick your nose?
Really?

Every time you touch me the world dissolves.
Your sweet embrace,
the only warmth in a world of bitter ice,
our love will last
forever
…which was actually two weeks.
You said he was your ex.
No, no, I don't want a threesome.

Every time you touch me the world dissolves.
The taste of your lips,
heroin for my soul.
My breath in yours, our bodies are one
forever
…which was actually a year.
Heroin for my soul, not real heroin.
No, I'm not selling my television for your fix.

Every time I touch me the world dissolves.
Ecstasy made flesh in five fingers.
No one knows me like I do
and my imagination knows no bounds.
I am complete
forever.

Miss Smith's Upgrade

A. E. Churchyard

"Miss... Smith?"

"That's me." I waved my hand from amongst the rows of women in the waiting room.

"If you'll follow me, please." The nurse beckoned me over with her clipboard.

Following her down the corridor, I passed thirty or so doors before she opened one. "Take a seat, please. The Doctor will be with you momentarily."

I stepped into what looked like a standard therapy room. In the centre of it, stood a reclining treatment chair with its robotic arms in rest pose. It was the only place to sit in the whole room; even the control panel was attached to a standing desk.

I walked over to it. The air passing my face smelled of strawberry and citrus. *Those are my favourite scents. The room's AI must be trying to put me at ease.* Stopping beside the chair, I stared down at the shiny, plastic-looking cushions and laid one hand on the arm.

The chair whirled into life, the robotic arms sweeping up out of 'rest' and into 'standby', the slim metal fingers poised in the air. I jumped back. *There are all those stories... people ripped to pieces by a malfunctioning chair or held down while the doctor does unspeakable things to them. Do I really want to do this?*

"It won't hurt you, you know."

The voice came from behind me and I turned too quickly, losing my balance and stumbling against the chair. One of the robot arms caught me, and the feel of the cold metallic hand on my bare upper arm drew a shriek of fear from my lungs.

"Chair, standby." The doctor rushed forward and helped me stand on both feet again as the chair let go of me. "Try not to panic, Miss Smith, the arms react to your emotions."

I nodded silently.

"According to your notes, this is the first time you've needed any form of treatment. I'll deactivate the arms for the moment so you can relax and answer my questions." She tapped out a sequence on the control panel and the arms dropped into rest mode again. "Take a seat."

I settled onto the chair gingerly, shooting nervous glances at my surroundings and avoiding looking at the chair's arms.

The doctor tapped another sequence out and my medical records rolled up on the wall screen. "I see that you have the standard memory implant and profession chip. And that neither has been updated since you moved to The City. Can I ask why?"

I shrugged. "I didn't see the need to have it done. They were installed in the old-fashioned way in the Town Hospital and I had figured that I'd get them done when I went back home next year."

"I see." The doctor scrolled through my DNA profile and antibody levels. "You're in superb physical shape. Ever experienced any of the Mood Enhancers that they offer next door?"

Next door to the Treatment Clinic, sat the flashing lights and loud music of the Mood Factory. I'd heard that you could experience almost anything in there, virtually of course, and that the Mood Enhancers could take your mind to places that you could only dream about.

I shook my head. "I had a strict upbringing."

"Good. Those things always complicate these sorts of procedures. What about virtual games?" she said.

"I didn't even know that VR existed until I moved here. Oh, I played the normal Two-D games, but Mama hated the idea of us sullying our implants with the VR jacks," I replied, shifting on the conformable plastic under me.

"Fair enough. I see that you have been given a five-slot Upgrade Credit via your profession. You currently only use one. What would you like me to add in?" She looked at me.

I blushed.

She grinned. "New Boyfriend?"

I nodded, unable to form the words I needed to say for the records the AI was making.

"You are going to have to say something, you know… I know how embarrassing it can be the first time that you do this, but it can only be done if you request it verbally; it acts as the first stage of consent." The doctor seemed amused at my reticence.

I swallowed. "My Boyfriend suggested that I get a Libido Upgrade."

"That's a fairly standard request; I hear it about nine times a week from various ages of all genders." She pressed a key and the wall screen showed a list of Upgrades that would fit in my implant. "As long as he's not coercing you to do it in some way…"

"Oh, he's not," I replied, unable to stop myself laughing. "I suggested that he get an empathy level check if I did the upgrade."

The doctor raised an eyebrow. "Is he?"

"He had it done yesterday. Told me this morning that he was sorry that he'd upset me and that I didn't have to go through with it." I looked up at the screen. "Hmm. I think I'll have the 700. He's a natural 800, so that will mean I'll at least be able to keep up with him."

"Are you sure that you want this?" The doctor was suddenly very serious. "You already have a natural 300 so that upgrade will make you the one to keep up with, not the other way round."

I thought about all the times he'd initiated sex and I'd backed off. *Why am I having this done anyway? There's nothing wrong with my natural libido speed.* I scanned through the options. *I have a natural 300 so I really only need a 400 to keep up with him.*

"Maybe, I should have the 400 instead then?" I couldn't keep the question out of my tone.

"Why are you with him?" she asked, leaning on the desk and looking at me intently.

I thought about it. "He's the first man to be interested in who I am since I moved here. I read paper books, listen to music that is over five hundred years old and try not to use my implants or the computer more than I have to, to do my job. I've been told that I'm living archaeology because I come from a town that still teaches kids without using their memory implants and most people like to get out in the fresh air and countryside to relax."

"What's he like?"

"Tall, dark-haired and blue-eyed. Handsome and strong. His parents chose his physicality before he was born. He's high IQ and an Upper Heir, tattoo and everything." I sighed. "I'm from the complete opposite of his world." I swallowed the tears that clogged up my throat for a moment before continuing, "He's funny in an old-fashioned, goofy way. He likes to explore the parts of the city that his class don't usually go anywhere near, just because I have to work there. He meets me for lunch and we take it in turn to pay. He holds my hand when we go into his part of the city to reassure me that he's with me. I suppose he's just slumming it with me, but I can't help hoping that the relationship goes somewhere, so I'm trying my damnedest to make it work."

The doctor stood up. "I'm going to let you into a secret."

I looked at her.

"The higher levels of these upgrades," she waved one hand at the wall screen, "will turn you into his wildest dream. But it won't keep him with you. He's interested in you because you are the way you are. You think that changing yourself will make him happy, but all he really needs is a wakeup call."

"What on earth do you mean?"

She pressed a key on the console. "This was your vitals while you were talking about him."

I dutifully watched the graphs and numbers bounce around on the wall screen before asking, "What does it mean, though?"

"You love him for who he is now, not what his parents made him. He went ahead and had that Empathy level check, and even got it topped up because he didn't want to lose you. You're doing the same thing for him; getting a Libido Upgrade so that you can make him feel the way he makes you feel." The doctor threw her hands up in the air. "All very commendable, but you both need to get out of The City."

I stared at her. "What do you suggest?"

"Take him to meet your parents. I suppose you've met his?"

I nodded.

"Get him out of his comfort zone and see what happens. Come back to me if he's still with you and you still want to indulge him by doing it." She tipped her head to one side. "Or you could add a 300 and see if it makes a difference between you. They're easily exchangeable after all."

I stared at my feet. *She's right.*

The silence lengthened until the AI spoke. "Doctor, your next patient will be escorted to you in five minutes. That's just enough time to perform a single upgrade."

The stilted voice shocked me out of my dream of taking him home. I licked my lips. "Okay. I'll take the 300 and I'll do as you suggest as well."

"Fair enough." The doctor smiled at me. "Lie down on the chair with your head in the hoop of the headrest. You're anxious enough about the process that I can authorise a sedative to help you relax. It won't take long."

I did as she instructed, breathed in deeply when the mask covered my nose and mouth and dozed off as the robotic arms came to life above me.

When I woke up, the doctor was still smiling. She helped me out of the chair and gave me a cup of water to clear the dryness from my throat caused by the sedative. "How'dya feel?"

I moved my head a little. Nothing seemed to have changed. I said as much.

"Think about your boyfriend."

I pictured his deep blue eyes and smooth coffee-coloured skin and felt my body come alive at just the thought of his hands touching me. "Ooh." My nipples tingled. "That's a lot faster than normal."

"Good, it's working."

I took a deep breath. "What happens if I do everything you suggested and he still leaves me?"

She patted my shoulder as she led me to the door. "In that case you need to get yourself a boyfriend upgrade. Find someone who will care for you as much as you do for them."

"Thank you." The door swished open to reveal the nurse and my boyfriend.

"There you are!" He threw his arms around me and I felt my body respond. "You were in here so long that I thought something bad had happened... you hear so many bad stories."

As he guided me down the corridor, I heard the nurse say to the doctor:

"Did it work?"

The doctor replied, "I hope so. We have so few pure humans left that saving her was a priority... and the only way to do that was to ensure that she found her Love. It's not something that can be programmed or upgraded after all."

Cake & Quill

I Dream Of Rigor: A Heartwarming Tale Of Murder, Sex, And Snuggling

W.D. Frank

My breath becomes heavy as I watch the blood run from my reflection's powdered nostrils. An eager female voice calls from beyond the reinforced bathroom door; I ignore her, instead opting to caress the blade of the sword in my hand. Oh, I totally forgot to introduce myself. My name is Frank Jensen and as you have no doubt gathered, I like killing people... a lot. I am not sure why I am so hopelessly fixated on death, but I have been this way since I was a child. I can't explain it. The act of taking a human's life is exciting enough, but the most beautiful part comes after it has been taken. Once they have faded, I become the owner of the shell that once contained their soul. I mean, don't get me wrong. I always have to dispose of my possessions sooner than later, but sometimes I keep them at my side for a few days. We watch movies together. We dine together. We fall asleep in each other's arms. It's truly beautiful. Death unites people like few things can. It turns enemies into close friends, annoying comedians into lovely mutes, and ex-girlfriends into tea party companions. I reluctantly wipe the blood and cocaine from my nose before replying to my thieving girlfriend's lusty pleas with a vulgar command.

"Bend your ass over, Doris! I am coming out!"

I lift the katana over my head and dash into the bedroom, shrieking Japanese battle-cries like a madman. I immediately locate my startled little Doris. She is sprawled out on the sleek white bedsheets with a dumbstruck expression on her face and two fingers in her cunt. I slap the flat of the blade against my thigh and burst into a fit of shrill laughter.

"What the fuck, Frank!? You scared the flying shit out of me! Where did you even get that sword!?"

I titter at the question and gently lay my head on Doris' breasts, resisting the call of tranquility as her immaculately smooth skin meets my blazing cheeks. "I found it in the living room before you got here. Apparently, the owner of this place is freaking awesome."

Doris seems to take this confession as one of my humorously narcissistic remarks. She runs a hand through my hair and smiles sweetly as she whispers her barbed reply, "You are such a nerdy little sissy. What's up with you and snuggling?"

I rub my face across her like an adorable cat and place the katana on the bed. "I don't know, James Franco. I like feeling connected to you, I guess."

I bite my tongue as I realize I just committed the horrific blunder of saying another person's name during a moment of love and lust. Fortunately, Doris doesn't seem to take offense. She simply continues to stroke my head and offer loving whispers. I feel my hands tighten around the handle of the katana as she grabs my penis with her other hand. I shed a few odd tears in the midst of my drug-induced euphoria and look into the innocent blue eyes of my lover. She always wears such an affectionate smile on her face when she pleasures me. It's no wonder that I so often let my guard down with this woman. She feels like my... Fuck! The realization horrifies me. My head leaps from her lap and I stare intently at the ivory hand around my dick. "You..." I giggle impishly as the words begin to escape my mouth. I can't tell her. The thought is sick enough in my own head. "You are the most perfect woman I ever met."

I relax back onto her chest and fight back a frown as my whole body trembles. Sometimes I wonder if we reveal our darkest secrets to ourselves during intimate moments like these. If so, should I feel silly for being ashamed of what I see? Killing another human being doesn't bother me. Why should I be scared of my feelings?

Doris' soothing voice abruptly interrupts my thought process.

"Do you like this, Frank?"

I grit my teeth and slide the cold steel of the blade against her stomach. "Yes, I like it very much. Don't stop for the sword. Keep going, darling. You have me."

My partner is bizarrely unfazed by the fact that there is a sword pressed against her stomach. I silently curse her conveniently overwhelming stupidity and raise the weapon until it is touching her nipples. Christ, why do women always make murder so easy for me? I grumble at my unspoken inquiry. My arms and neck are starting to ache, however, the sight of steel against Doris' body is enough incentive for me to ignore it. Unfortunately, I cannot do much harm to her in this horrid position.

"Do you want me to fuck you or not?"

Doris laughs as soon as the question leaves my lips.

"Well, yeah! Are we done with the goddamn snuggling?"

I remove myself from the bed and admire her perfect form for what I intended to be the last time.

"Just get on your knees and point your ass this way."

She chuckles and spreads her legs as wide as she can.

"Put the sword away first. I don't want you to involve that in our sexy moments anymore. I mean, it's kind of hot, but fucking around with deadly weapons is just asking for trouble."

I do as she says and toss the badass murder weapon

onto the carpet. I could have just killed her right there and then, but suddenly sex seems really important. Her death can wait until after we are both satisfied. After all, the owner of this house isn't ever coming back.

Parsley, Sage, Rosemary and Skunk Cabbage

Tina Rath

I'll send my love a posy sweet upon his wedding day
That he may wear it in his coat, so gallant and so gay,
Of Slighted Love and Blighted Love, set round a faded rose
And then a ring of Ruined Maid - he always fancied those.

And for his bride I'll weave a wreath: sweet scented Love is Blind
And rue, and yew and Bleeding Heart, and Poor Girl Used Unkind,
And Pity Me, and Sweet Love Lost and crimson Left to Shame
And if they have a happy day - well I won't be to blame.

Man in a Can

Chloe Hammond

Although I don't smoke anymore, I still do that silly run that doesn't get you anywhere faster than walking to grab a newly vacated table outside the freshly revamped wine bar / bistro Elle and I have adopted as our second home this month. Our friendly waitress, who sometimes slips us a double while charging for a single, sees me and waves. She finishes delivering another table's drinks and then comes over to take my order. Elle was right, a few hefty tips really do pay for themselves in service later. I swallow a smirk when a table of bright young things huff and scowl as the waitress walks straight past their arrogantly waved twenty-pound notes.

"Black coffee, lots of sugar and an extra shot. Pint of tap water, no ice, and a double vodka and full fat coke, please." I am still paying for last night's extravagances. I may feel fit to graduate to fruit juices once I've rehydrated and fired up my cylinders with excessive caffeine. Elle, however, will bowl straight into vodka. I don't know how she does it. She will also look just-out-of-bed tousled, and grubbily dishevelled in a 'take me to bed and ravish me' way. Whereas I have looked in a mirror and know I just look, well, trashed. Even freshly-washed hair and lashings of mascara have not been enough to revitalise me. Youth Dew my arse.

"So, where is she then?" asks our tame waitress as she plonks my pint of water in front of me. I'm so predictable. She knows I'll grab and glug it down first before shakily reaching for the four little sachets of sugar beside my coffee cup. I think she may have a little crush. I think that may be why she risks her job by bringing us the extra-large drinks. I won't discourage her. Elle is very liberal in her tastes; she just likes sex.

"Elle? God knows, but her drink is on the table now, so she should arrive any second," I say, grinning. And speak of the devil, guess who I spot sauntering down the sunny street towards us. The only sign she may be a little worse for wear is the huge pair of sunglasses she's wearing. As she approaches us, she pushes them onto her head and smiles mischievously.

"Who's taking my name in vain?" she asks, plonking herself opposite me, and taking a massive gulp of her drink. The waitress shakes herself awake from the hypnotic trance Elle's swaying hips and merrily bouncing tits had induced. "Two more of these, please," Elle asks her, winking lasciviously.

People often ask if we are sisters because we are both pale, with green eyes and big breasts and we laugh all the time we are together. We don't actually look alike at all. I am Irish pale, with skin that turns to corned beef at the first sign of a breeze, whereas she has the porcelain skin of the Polish. Officially, according to women's magazines, and other such oracles of truth, I have the better figure of the two of us. Elle has a massive arse, and her legs are shorter than mine, but she is much, much sexier than I am.

She laughs all the time because she is self-assured and full of wicked thoughts; I laugh because I'm anxious and usually serious and so happy to be in the company of this goddess. You might wonder why we are friends, two such different women, but we complement each other. When the gaping maw of her insecurity roars, I understand and listen to the things she would never tell anyone else. And when the rage bubbles over my daily mask of politeness, she is there to hear me, and laugh with me, and finally dance me out of the doldrums.

Her real name is Elizabeth, and everyone else knows her as Beth. I was introduced to her as Elle when we worked together, because there was a stuck-up cow called Beth already working there when she started, so she had decided to be known as Elle to avoid being confused with the bitch, and Liz just wouldn't do. Now we don't work together anymore, I still call her Elle, which confuses all her other friends, and new work colleagues, but to me she will always be Elles Belles.

"How was he?" I ask as she slides a cigarette between her quirked lips, inhaling deeply. The scent of freshly-lit tobacco always stirs the want in me, so I pause to breathe the fresh smoke in. I gave up smoking when I discovered the first sign of a crease developing in my upper lip, highlighted into a trench by harsh morning sunlight. So no matter how much I might fancy a drag, I don't. Elle is a year older than me, and smokes twice as much as I ever did. She has no lines at all.

"Alright." She blows out another stream of bluish smoke, cigarette held between two long-nailed, purple-polished fingers. "He was humping away, but it wasn't really getting either of us anywhere, so I flipped him over, jumped on, and finished myself off. I asked him if he was going to come anytime soon, and he said he didn't think so, so I climbed back off, and went to sleep. I think he expected a replay this morning, but nah, couldn't be bothered, so I sent him on his way with his morning glory intact." She flicks her ash dismissively.

"Thanks, love," she purrs. The waitress is back, putting our drinks in front of us. Elle lowers her sun glasses to smoulder at her a little. She wants the extra vodkas to start flowing. I'm not sure I can manage vodka yet, so I ask for a large orange juice.

Elle doesn't lower her voice, or her raucous guffaws while she recounts her exploits, and even as I cringe slightly as the bright young things glare over, I glory in her ability to ignore them, and belly laugh too. A little bit of me feels sorry for the older man Elle had met the night before; he'd followed her home like a happy puppy, believing all his Christmases had come at once. But at the same time I think of all the times men have humped themselves to happiness on me, and then rolled over and gone to sleep, without the manners to even offer to help me out, and I laugh out loud, conceding she has just served a man-sized dish of own medicine.

"What happened with you and what's his face, Jake?"

"George? Nothing, bleurgh. He was married," I judder at the memory of his predictable tales of not being understood.

"Hmmm, so you still haven't broken your dry spell? Come on, you need to get laid, what's wrong with you?"

"There's nothing wrong with me, I'm just fussy." I don't mean to insult her, I am fussy, too fussy. I won't sleep with men with wives, or bad shoes, or unevenly sized nostrils, or too much body hair, or silly laughs, or boring jobs, the list goes on. Her face, however, has flinched in surprised hurt. "No, no," I hurry to reassure her. "It's not a good thing to suddenly find a man repulsive because he flashes cartoon socks when he crosses his legs. I know I need to be less picky, I'm sure I am turning down perfectly nice men; it's just that my head and my lady bits don't seem to be connected, so while my head says, give him a chance, it's not his fault his accent makes your teeth ache, listen to what he's saying, he's a nice man who works helping people with Alzheimer's. But my foo just says no, and shuts up shop, and he gets relegated to my friend list."

Elle sucks her teeth at me and shakes her head, offence forgotten in despair at my predicament. You see, while Elle loves being single, the thrill of the chase, the adventure, the exploration of the unknown, I hate it. I am

only single because I can't find anyone I fancy.
"How's the online dating going?" she asks hopefully.
I wrinkle my nose and shake my head.
"They're all such liars." I sip more of my juice. My blood sugars seem to be evening out a bit, and combined with the caffeine I'm feeling almost human again. "I got one reply that seemed interesting this week, but when he rang me, he sounded older than he'd said in his reply, but I thought, no, give him a chance, he may just have a sore throat. Then he confessed to being in his sixties. That's more than twenty years older than me. How is that ok? And he had the audacity to get all offended and rude when I wouldn't agree to a date."
"Cheeky fucker," agrees Elle.
"I had an idea the other day. Someone should invent 'Man In A Can'. Like the advert – does exactly what it says on the tin."
"Oo! Yes, 'Man In A Can', fabulous idea. The convenience. Today I feel like a blond, with surfer dude sensibilities, and body, pop him out, let him roger me senseless, and then pop him back in his tin, onto the shelf, until I feel like that flavour again."
"That wasn't what I meant. I meant that you could read the ingredients, and the description, and know exactly what you were getting, no more lies or falsehoods, no more surprise novelty boxer shorts, or right wing tendencies. But now you come to mention it, yes, I suppose the convenience could be a selling point too."
"Yes," she muses, lighting another cigarette. "Ingredients and a description, excellent idea, tonight I want a dark-haired poetic type, to sing me his lyrics and beg me to be his muse in the moonlight." Elle sighs happily at the image.
"It would stop agonising situations like when I met up with that guy who described himself as medium build,

and talked about playing football, but looked like Penfold, from Danger Mouse, and had blatantly never done any sport or exercise in his life. He had photoshopped his photo, a lot," I continue, but Elle isn't listening any more; two men have just walked out of the pub with their drinks and are stood shoulder to shoulder scanning for somewhere to sit. One of them has floppy dark hair, and a Hugh Grant in Bridget Jones' Diary air. His purple shirt is well cut, and his grey trousers look expensive, if a little shiny.

"Oh, hello," she croons, blowing out smoke ostentatiously, so it causes her lips to pout, while her chin tips to expose her long creamy throat. The man catches sight of her and freezes for a moment as she raises her cigarette back to her glossy lips and sucks suggestively while gazing at him through lowered lashes, then he lights his own cigarette, and smoulders right back at Elle.

"Oh yes, he'll do, he'll do nicely," she mutters, wriggling in her seat. She reminds me of a leopard giving one last squirm before it pounces. "And he's got a friend for you too, look."

Yes, I've seen his friend. He is wearing a suit. I don't like suits, make shit bodies look good. And he has slicked his hair back and to one side in an attempt to hide how much it is thinning. Why don't men just get it clipped short? It looks so much better. His shoes are those strange elongated Rumpelstiltskin pointy slip-ons that so many city chaps wear. I hate them. I remember the advice to avoid men with slip-on shoes, even if they are trendy slip-on shoes.

Aware that we are looking in his direction, he starts to peacock, flick flacking his tie and throwing back his head to laugh, pulling his lips back and exposing big white teeth, so he looks like he is taking big bites of air and chewing it, rather than sharing merriment. He honks like a goose. The hand not flipping his tie around is in holster position, pelvis thrust forward. He looks to his friend for permission to proceed. Hugh-Grant-Alike chucks his fag butt onto the floor and grinds it out with the heel of his very pointy, very patent, but at least lace up, shoe. He saunters over with Chuckles bringing up the rear.

"Hello ladies, may we join you?" Elle languidly gestures for them to be seated. A bitter bit of me can't help wondering which he is most interested in, us or the two spare seats at our table. I shut the sharp little voice up. Elle likes her suitor, so I need to play nice. I'll have to find a way of keeping mine at arm's length, while not insulting him to the point where he leaves, taking his friend with him. I suspect this is going to be a challenge. He has sat on the side of the table at a close right angle to me, bashing my knees with his and kicking my ankles with his stupid pointy shoes, so I have no choice but to slide my seat backwards and wrap my ankles around my chair legs.

As he sets his sights on me, I can see his eyes are already beer-glazed, thickening his already crocodile skin. He is going to be difficult to deter, he's going to be one of those ones that feels that just because his friend is in luck, he should be too. I reach over for the vodka Elle bought me earlier; it's gone a bit warm in the last of the evening sun, but I think I'm going to need it. Chuckles leans across the corner of the table to impart his name into my ear, setting all the drinks wobbling, and blasting me with Southern Comfort fumes and bits of spit. Southern Comfort breath always smells like vomit to me.

I smile grimly away from him, moving my nose as far from his stench as possible. Ignoring him bluntly, I ponder how another bonus with a man in a can would be how you could force this calamity back into his can if you accidentally opened it. I finish my vodka and look around for the waitress to order more.

It's going to be a long night.

Metamorphosis

Angelika Rust

"Steve," she says.

My features morph into wood. Smooth and polished.

I nod, as if to confirm I remember. Of course I remember. I wasted more than a year of my life on that guy.

"That time when he came to my place every noon," she continues.

I nod again. He used to come home for lunch breaks. Quite the drive, but nevertheless, he did. To see me. And then, suddenly, he stopped, and went to her place instead. It was a shorter way, he told me. More time to relax during the break.

"He always wanted to get cozy. I wasn't having any of that. Well, a bit. But I always drew the line when he wanted to sleep with me."

My features morph into stone. Chiseled and rigid.

"I know," I reply.

I don't. I'm a liar.

"Really? How can you know?" She sounds like she believes me.

"I'm not entirely stupid."

I am. I trusted you.

"Well, I'm glad. You know, not sleeping with him, I've never proved myself a truer friend to anyone."

She leaves.

My features morph into wax. Soft and runny.

My face melts.

"A true friend," I tell the shadow of her memory, that lingers on, "would have told me there and then."

Agnés and Albertine

Charlotte Stirling

The Eastern sky lit up for hours this time. Smoke billowing out of whatever building had been bottle-bombed and the stench of charred meat reaching for the wind. Cajoling it to carry the warning to every survivor still making their way towards a pre-recorded radio message or following hopeful, dusty signs carved into tree trunks and telephone poles.

Hope was one of the biggest killers this side of *La Grande Peste*, as Albertine insisted on calling it. She thought it lent a romantic quality to the destruction of mankind, made it easier reading, so to speak.

Agnés thought it ridiculous but didn't have the heart to say. People took things much harder now there wasn't much warmth in the world. There wasn't much law and order either, so unless you wanted a knife in your guts or a rifle butt in your cunt, you kept quiet and as small as you could. Edging along the corners of the world, finding comfort in dark places, silent places.

Albertine had worked for Agnés at a high-end milliner just off Rue Saint-Roch in Paris. She had the most delicate of fingers, capable of tiny, sensuous movements that could make silk sing and lace renounce its own mother.

In the early days, she had felt quite possessive of this remarkable talent and later, when they became lovers, she became *possessive* of something else entirely.

'Do you think that's Marseille?' Agnés asked, pointing towards the spark-filled, Eastern sky. 'Because

if it is, we should think about increasing our radius.'
Albertine watched the sky seriously. Every choice she made, whether it was between a creamy *Vichyssoise* or a succulent *Langoustine* or which tender piece of Agnés to kiss first, was weighed and measured, handled and inhaled until she was absolutely sure.

'I think we should keep going straight, Cherie. That last message was very clear about the date. If we don't reach the port by the 23rd, we could miss the boat.'

Agnés shut her mouth quickly to bite off an angry noise that screamed below her surface. *That putain boat*.

Ever since Albertine had first heard the message on her wind-up radio, she had begun to obsess about this unlikely boat and a way back home to Senegal. Every night and morning, Albertine would check the date in her notebook, its pages grubbed and marked.

'Cherie,' Agnés ventured, 'we have no idea if this boat is real, if the message is still relevant or even if it is safe? We have come so far, too far to screw it all up now for an unknown quantity. Please be reasonable.'

'Reasonable?' Albertine's voice sharpened at its edges.

'You think it is unreasonable for me to try to find a way back to my home? To see if any of my family are still alive? This plague has left me with nothing. What is the point of living even, if it means we give up the search?'

Agnés frowned at her lover of two decades.

'You don't have nothing. You have me. And that's not what I meant at all. But we could be sacrificing ourselves to any kind of bad things. They could be Eaters for all we know. Please, Cherie, please, think more logically. You haven't been back to Africa since you were nine years old. You are now fifty-eight; how many people do you think are alive there still? I don't mean to be unkind, but the reality is that no one is left.'

Albertine scowled; her skin, the colour of Habana cigars, creased a thousand ways. Eyes that had once entranced Agnés with their sparkle and significance now seemed smaller. Resentment shrank Albertine's beauty and magnified her flaws; continual hardship did the rest.

'She had been so beautiful,' Agnés thought sadly, 'skin like midnight glass, breath that frosted the air with cassis and a cunt so warm and muscled it was a divine, marvelous thing.'

Agnés remembered her first sight of Albertine, one January morning. The Frost moon had smiled icily and Paris was transformed into a playground of dusting sugar and splendor.

Agnés had been working late on a wedding hat for a politician's wife. A cheap woman whose face and name had become defined by the greasy wealth of her husband.

The hat was magnificent with layers of the lightest dove grey, fine-weave straw and curls of smoky chiffon that competed for space like drunken acrobats. It was far too good for *Madame le Bourgeois,* but Agnés had learned something valuable years ago. To keep her mouth shut when the bad words came and only open it to let the complimentary ones out.

Madame was delighted but had left a dreadfully cheap tip to Agnés's disgust and she wished that she had left five sharp pins in the lining. Humming softly, Agnés began to turn the lights down and clear her workbench of the Swarovski crystals that littered the surface, winking sadly in the fading light.

Agnés was locking the safe when she heard several thumps followed by a string of curses both in English and French. The English was tinged with those long American vowels that linger determinedly and the French blessed with the honeyed ones of Africa's West Coast. There was a brushing of skirts and a strong rap on the shop's front door. Agnés remembered feeling quite cross at the interruption and had muttered, 'Salope', under her breath as she pulled the door open and fell immediately in love.

But she wasn't in love anymore and the reality of this two-dimensional world, this black and tan world, put all relationships under excruciating pressure. Emotions were as hard and useless as diamonds, a suffocating luxury in a society that survived on petrol, antibiotics and flesh.

Albertine had begun to repulse her. Things that had been so tender and enduring were now rancid and run to fat. The curvy lines of her *Rubenesque Noir* had blurred into *lardons* and those treacle and russet eyes that were sent from heaven had turned to *porc boue.*

A sick, orange light had perpetuated the skyline for weeks and the sooty, screaming wind bit and toyed, bullying leaves into submission. A nerve-shredding howling and the sheer strength of the Mistral wind would leave songbirds dead under snapped trees; dozens of them lying broken and soft in the aftermath of a wind with a legend.

The Mistral was so famous in France for affecting the mind that certain *crimes passionelles* were pardoned. It played tricks on a person, blowing papers across the room, making hinges squeak and hallways moan.

The women trudged on acutely aware of each other and of their stench. But now, instead of walking closely together for comfort and warmth, they began to drift apart, sometimes rounding corners without each other in sight, sighs of both frustration and relief when a greyed head or a hunched pair of shoulders came back into view.

They stopped at the foot of *Les Alpes,* magnificent mountains leading to Italy and Switzerland. High, granite-faced marvels with air as pure as a first confirmation, they towered above the travellers. Their range and snowy tops beyond imagination, and Agnés felt a surge of hope and of determination. Her head was full of buzzing, like cholera or jubilant horse flies, and she needed to clear it and convince Albertine to forget the fucking boat.

'That,' Agnés said, pointing towards the mountains, 'is where we must go if we want to survive. Villages are surprisingly hardy and the cold might have held off infection. Think of the fresh milk and bread. They might have bread! Don't you think, Bertie?' Agnés was so excited that she missed the darkness that stole across her lover's face. And then, through clenched and painful lips, Albertine spoke precisely.

'No. We must get to the port. That is the plan. That is what we decided to do. You promised, you promised a hundred times. I won't let you take this away from me.'

Agnés spoke without turning her face from the green slopes and snowy tips further up.

'And *I* am not going to entertain this madness anymore. It is stupidity. It is selfish and it is going to get us killed.'

She heard a tiny movement behind her and spun round to find Albertine standing a few feet away holding a jagged, killing stone. A stone big enough to cave in a woman's skull, a stone that had seen blood before. Agnés was frightened, so she pretended ignorance to Albertine's killing stone and suggested they camp there, in the foothills, and make decisions about their future in the morning.

Albertine nodded and a jittery peace presided over their supper of hard cheese and flatbread. There were even a couple of slices of a soft and wrinkled apple, still sweet enough to delight the mouth.

All talk of the future was avoided as they made each

other tea from the herb bags they both carried, having become adept at foraging for plants and roots now that pharmacies were obsolete. You could often tell how dangerous a plant was by its name. Hammerfall, Bloodwell and Devil's Arse, for example. But not always. Enchanté, Serenity and Venus Mater were all deadly too.

Agnés had become obsessed with collecting dried willow bark after breaking into a deserted Library and finding out that it contained salicin. A drug that could pull down fevers and relieve moderate pain. Albertine remembered that Agnés had danced in the aisles, waving the book in the air as she boasted, 'at least *le sale grippe* won't finish us off'.

She had looked so pretty, her auburn hair still bright and without a trace of grey, blue eyes a little faded but brimming with enthusiasm. Even in her *Costume de Peste,* filthy men's trousers held up by braces made for a rugby player and a frayed, paisley shirt that Albertine had stolen for her from a farmer's washing line back in the Loire valley, Agnés seemed so vital.

Albertine had never loved Agnés. Oh! She had liked her very much; especially her wit, the skin at the nape of her neck, even the two freckles on her arse that would bloom when licked. But mostly for the protection a middle-class French woman could afford to a well-used thirty-year-old African Immigrant with no papers. Agnés gave her a cover but also shelter, food, water and security.

The *petite bourgeoisie* in Paris were vicious, using their language and cadence to stab and bruise the bemused Albertine. There was no sun in Paris for the newly-arrived African girl; just dark and dangerous corners, and the relief at the security that Agnés offered made the sex feel hardly a burden at all.

Albertine preferred to fuck men. She liked their

strength, the rusty graze of a forearm across her bare shoulders; she liked their girth and length. She enjoyed inhaling the salty Camembert smell of their *couilles* after a lunchtime shower.

But men frightened Albertine and they had hurt her many times. Broken bones and smiles, walking and wincing to the dyspeptic street doctor at *Porte de Clignancourt* for a shot of penicillin and another tube of pain medication.

When Albertine had arrived in France she was nine years old. A beautiful, well-developed child who entranced some men so entirely they ignored her young age and concentrated only on fulfilling their sick desires. She had been raped countless times by a certain type of man and, with each violation, a little bit of her compassion whittled away. Albertine used her hate well and had committed murder five times in her life, a fact she had never shared with Agnés.

As they went to sleep that night, at opposite ends of the fire, they eyed each other warily, becoming jumpy and anxious in the twilight. Alert to every snapping twig, owl hoot and the death shrieks of small creatures, the women quickly became exhausted.

Albertine was the first to surrender to sleep, helped along by the strong herbal sedative that Agnés had dissolved in her tea.

Agnés rose before dawn, resting only a few hours to refresh herself. After all, the mountainous terrain would require extra effort and the air would thin quickly.

Albertine slept on as Agnés broke camp, her breathing even and calm, and as her face relaxed, her youth seemed to spring back in like a well-risen *mochatine*, giving Agnés brief pause as she walked softly towards her lover, the killing stone in her hand.

Once it was done, once Albertine was somewhere

better, Agnés covered her body with rocks and solemnity. It took a good few hours and broke well into her morning but it was important for Agnés to mark Albertine's death with something solid and lasting.

When the last stone was placed, Agnés collected both rucksacks and tied the two together with a couple of old belts and a corded piece of blue rope. Things that Albertine had stolen for them – she had always been a skillful thief. Swinging the bags onto her back, Agnes never looked back at the makeshift grave, her mourning had been swift and fierce in the cold dawn.

The sky blazed azure, a hot, excitable blue, and happiness pulsed through her veins. Agnés felt herself lifted as hope billowed around her heart. As she grasped her walking stick, a slight tremor shook her left hand. She flexed it twice to loosen any stiff tendons, unaware that Albertine's herbal poison had started its slow, remorseless journey around her body.

The Number

Bradley Darewood

For a good time call 620-876-0212.

Peter stared at the writing scrawled on the wall of the squalid restroom for far too long. He was constipated, but that was beside the point. He was lonely. sitting on the toilet of Hawerth Park, he should have been revolted by the piss smell and the broken toilet seat, but instead he was lonely. The idea of a "good time" tugged at his heart (and, well, a certain other organ) and made him forget the homeless woman napping just on the other side of the stall door.

He should really wipe and leave. He should pull his pants up and go. But…

Peter reached into his pocket and pulled out his cell phone.

6.2.0.8.7.6.0.2.1.2.

Peter's heart raced as he heard the phone ring. *Please don't be a tranny. Please don't be a tranny. Please don't--*

"Hello?" The voice on the other side of the line was sweet and musical like a birdcall on a summer's day.

"I-- um--" Peter realized he had no idea what to say.

"Who-- who is this?" An angry storm swept the sweetness from the summer-like voice.

"I'm Peter. W--" *Would you like to have a good time?* "W-We… we met the other day and…"

"I don't remember any Peter."

"I-- I just thought we could have coffee."

Silence. Save for the snoring of the homeless woman. Peter couldn't breathe.

"Ok."

Oh my god, she said 'ok'! Peter's jaw dropped, paralyzed.

"Are you there?" The music was soft, cautiously returning.

"I-- yeah-- I'm here."

"Let's meet now."

"Now?"

"Yes. Now. Can you come to Café Laissez?"

"I-- yeah, it's across the street--"

"Where are you?"

"My--um-- my office--"

"See you in 15 minutes."

She hung up. Peter listened to the dial tone in shock.

Dazed, he slowly put his phone back into his pocket. *I have a date in fifteen minutes.* He wiped. *I have a date… IN FIFTEEN MINUTES!* Toilet paper stuck to his ass, Peter jumped off the toilet and pulled his pants up as fast as he could. They were stuck. He'd been eating a lot lately. He really should have bought new pants… or worn something with elastic. Taking a deep breath, he pulled as hard as he could. Finally! Buttoning them, he stumbled out of the bathroom.

He rushed to the sink, looking at himself behind the graffiti carved into the mirror. *God, I look like shit.* Burying his head in the sink, he soaked it, soaking his glasses in the process as well. He wiped them off on his shirt, then slicked his hair back. *Much better.*

Café Laissez-- that was all the way across the park. Peter leaped into a jog—well, with his jeans so tight, it was more of a waddle. He stopped to hold a tree, chest heaving. There was Café Laissez. He just had… to catch… his breath….

Peter took a seat on the patio and looked around. How

was he going to find her? Happy couples abounded, flirting over French pastries.

"Peter?"

Peter's head whipped up, knocking his glasses off kilter. *Good lord, she's... gorgeous.* Peter nearly choked on his own drool. Her blonde curls sparkled in the sunlight, her rosy cheeks warmed her smile. And that body. Good god, that *body.*

"Yes, uh--" *What's her name?* "I'm Peter."

The woman took a seat, her brow furrowed. "I really don't remember you at all."

"How did you know to find me?"

"You're the only one in the entire café sitting alone. And to be honest, you had an incredibly lost look about you."

"Yeah, I don't usually do this."

"Do what?"

"I mean I haven't been on a--" *No! Don't say that!* "...been to this café before."

"Remind me of where--"

"You were telling me about your profile--" Peter began.

"Profile? Like online dating? I'm not *that* lonely!"

Shit. I can't pretend to have met her online. Umm... "Well, to be fair, you were really drunk--"

She raised an eyebrow. "Drunk?"

Shit! This isn't going to work. There's no way this will work. Change the subject. "I mean it must have been on account of your ex--"

Rage made her eyes gleam. "That son of a bitch!" Her voice was guttural. Furious.

Peter was scared. Maybe bringing up the ex wasn't a good move. "I mean what an asshole." He bit his lip as he tried to commiserate.

"You have no idea."

"Yes, of course. I couldn't possibly relate. Men can be

so--"

"No, I mean you really have no idea."

"Excuse me?"

"You have no idea who I am."

"Of course I--"

She slammed her hands down on the table. "Where did we meet?"

"I--uh--we--"

"Do you even know my fucking name?"

"It's-- I--"

"Well?"

"Uh…. Sarah?"

"Jesus. Fucking. Christ."

"I just got your number and I thought--"

"It's him."

"Him?"

"I just, I can't even. I can't. That son of a bitch."

"I'm sorry. I just dialed the number and I thought you were gonna be gay or a tranny, but you're actually really hot and--"

"Wait, he told you I was gay?"

"No, I--"

"You… think I'm hot?"

Peter looked at her timidly… had the storm really passed that quickly? "Um… yeah. You're really hot."

"Really?"

"Really."

She bit her lip, her eyes looking him up and down. She looked almost… hungry.

Could she actually be aroused by his fat rolls? "I'm sorry I--"

"Do you want to come upstairs? My apartment's just upstairs from the café. Maybe we can… have tea."

She was staring at his crotch. At his *crotch*. At. His. *Crotch.*

"I-- um--" *Say "yes" you idiot!* "Of course."

The woman led Peter up the stairs to a small apartment. A Hello Kitty clock tick-tocked away in her living room, Hello Kitty pillows framed her couch. Peter moved to sit.

"The bedroom is this way."

Peter blushed. *This can't be happening. This is too good to be real.*

Her bedroom was small but immaculate. Cute even. Her sheets and pillows were a sort of tie-dyed pink. She grabbed him by the shirt and threw him on the bed.

"Shouldn't we--" Peter began.

She leapt on top of him, pulling his hands high above his head.

Click.

A hand cuff linked him to the bedpost.

"Woah! We just met! I'm not--"

Click.

The other hand was trapped as well.

"Tell me," she said, stroking the side of his face, "how do you know my ex-boyfriend?"

"I--I really don't know--"

"Hold on just one second."

She leaped off of him and sauntered out of the bedroom.

"Hey-- um--" Peter called after her, but she was gone.

He struggled with the handcuffs, to no avail. He really hadn't been on many dates. Well, any. But if he ever went on any future dates, he was sure one day he'd think this was the strangest date he'd ever been on.

Now that she was gone, he noticed the room had a distinct Clorox-smell to it. The woman liked her bleach.

She returned, standing in the bedroom doorway. "You know, I got a discount on this place. There's a mortuary just behind us. I guess most people don't like to live next to an incinerator for dead bodies."

"Uh... what?"

"Now, where were we?" Was that... a butcher knife in her hand? "How do you know my EX-BOYFRIEND!"

"Oh, Jesus!" Peter nearly choked.

"I have no idea how *on earth* he got so many of you to call! That *son of a bitch.*"

"You said he was a son of a bitch and I completely believe yo--"

"At first, I thought they were prank calls-- prank calls!"

"I really didn't mean to p--"

"But it was him! HIM! THAT SON OF A BITCH!"

"Okay, I really agree, I mean he--"

"Did he tell you that I'm *crazy?* Is that what he said?" She burnished the meat cleaver menacingly.

"I really never talked--"

"I'M NOT CRAZY!"

"Of course not."

"Did he tell you I have problems *holding my temper?* Did he tell you that?"

"I swear we never spoke--"

"I mean wouldn't you have anger problems if *he* was your boyfriend. EX-BOYFRIEND. I MEAN EX-BOYFRIEND! I DON'T WANT HIM TO BE MY BOYFRIEND. I HATE HIM! HATE HIM! HATE HIM!"

"I-- I'm really glad he's not my boyfri--"

"You know the first one hundred times-- *one hundred times*-- I just tried to blow it off. Hang up. But then..." She started pacing back and forth, slapping the cleaver on her hand. "But then I thought, 'How can I get back at these assholes if I just hang up?'"

"Oh my god." A sinking feeling gripped Peter by the nuts.

That Clorox smell. Her crazy rants. He eyed the sheets a little closer. Had they been... white? Was that tie-dye or were they... stains?

"How does he get *so many* of you? I mean he doesn't even have that many friends. He's an ASSHOLE. EVERYBODY HATES HIM."

"Yes, of course, I swear I hate him."

"You said you didn't know him."

"Of course not, I just hate him now. What an asshole."

"You're placating me."

"Of course not--"

"You think the men before you didn't try to placate me? That they wouldn't have said anything to get me to put down the knife?"

"How many men exactly have you…"

"You all think I'm *stupid!*"

"No! You're brilliant, I swear."

She brandished the butcher knife, blade knotted from deboning men.

"I really wish I'd never called that number--"

She shoved a cloth in his mouth.

"Mmmmm! Mmmm!!!"

"Should I let you go?"

"Mmmmm! Mmmm!!!"

"Give me one reason why!"

"Mmmmm! Mmmm!!!"

The butcher knife began its murderous arc.

Peter spit out the cloth. "Wait! I-- I can help you!"

"*Help* me?"

"I-- I can make the calls stop."

The woman paused. Her arm returned to her side, the butcher knife dangling from her fingers. "You can do that?"

"Yes! I just need a few minutes. I p-promise I'll--"

"Stop sputtering." She unlocked the handcuffs.

Peter gripped his reddened wrists in shock. "You're-- you're letting me go?"

"Jesus. Yes. Get out of here before I change my mind. If I get one more call, I swear to god I'm going to hunt you down and cut off your dick."

Peter raced out of the bedroom, past the Hello Kitty clock with its menacing tick tock. He sprinted down the stairs.

His chest was burning, heaving and wheezing like a beached whale. Sweat dripped from his face. But he didn't stop. He raced to the public restroom where this horrid sequence of events began just hours ago.

Peter stared at the toilet stall door and the number scrawled on it. Now what? He searched around for something he could use to scratch it out. He didn't dare leave the bathroom-- what if someone came in and called the number? Glumly, he pulled his keys out of his pocket. They would have to do.

He scraped and scraped until his hands bled. He'd barely made a dent on the number and his keys were getting filed smooth.

He sat on the toilet, defeated.

"Are you here to take a shit, mate, or are you just too fat to stand?" A British man with a bald head and blue track pants studied Peter from the entrance to the stall. His biceps bulged as he folded his arms. Tattoos wove their way out from underneath his tank top.

"I'm busy… doing something."

"Get the fuck out so I can take a shit."

"Go use the women's."

"Do I look like a bitch to you?"

Peter shut the stall door and resumed scratching at the number.

"For fuck's sake, what are you doing in there? I've got to take a shit and you're scratching at the wall like a rodent." The Brit shoved the door open.

"Hey!"

The man lifted Peter by his neck. "I thought I told you to get the fuck out of the toilet."

"You don't understand."

"Understand what?"

"There's a number--"

The man grinned. "A number?" He closed the stall door, pressed uncomfortably close to Peter as he studied the bathroom door. "A phone number," he said in satisfaction.

"Trust me, you don't want to call that number."

"Is it a bloke? I could really give a fuck, I haven't got any in days."

"No, it's not a man--"

"I could really use a 'good time' like it says here on the wall." The thug's eyes narrowed. "Is it your girlfriend, fat man?"

"No--"

He pulled out his phone. The melodic sound of numbers being entered into a phone echoed in the tiny public restroom. Peter's heart skipped a beat.

"Please, you've got to listen to me!"

"Shut up or I'll kick your sodding face in, mate." He squinted as he eyed the scratched numbers on the stall door. "I'm gonna call your girlfriend, and I'm gonna make her feel like a woman in ways your fat ass never could."

"She's not--"

"I told you to shut it, you fat fuck."

Peter started to protest, until the thought of the Brit being chopped into little pieces entered his mind.

"I can't make out that last number. You scratched it good, you little monkey."

Peter looked the man square in the eyes. The man who'd called him fat. And a monkey.

"It looks like… maybe…"

"It's a two."

The Chest

Tina Rath

"I never thought Dave would do it," Kelly wept. "Never. Never. Never."

"You told him to, babes," her friend, Caddy (short for Cadillac), measured a therapeutic dose of cold white wine into a glass and passed it to her, "you gave him the keys and told him to come and take anything he wanted."

"I never thought he'd *do* it though." Kelly took a mouthful of wine. "*And* he brought *her* with him."

"Course you didn't expect *that*, babes." Caddy filled her own glass. "You wanted him to come round on his own. Then you thought you'd get to talking about how you'd bought the stuff when you was all happy and lovey-dovey and one thing would lead to another, and off you'd go to bed, and it would be all happy and lovey-dovey again," she shook her head. "Wasn't going to happen, babes. Men aren't like us. Their minds just don't work that way. I wouldn't be surprised if you *had* gone off to bed, and afterwards he'd gone off with all your stuff all the same, so be thankful he did bring her along. I expect she made him. She's a bossy little cow."

She hitched herself onto the tall kitchen stool and began to rotate her left foot carefully, so many circles to the left, so many to the right. Then she did the same with the right one.

"What are you doing?" Kelly asked, momentarily distracted.

"My exercises. Slims the ankles and keeps the joints

supple." She stretched out both her admirably slim and no doubt supple ankles. "It works too. See."

Kelly, semi-hypnotised by the movement began to rotate her own left foot. Then she started to sob again. "They even took my chest…"

Startled, Caddy glanced at her friend's strappy top. Everything still seemed to be in place.

Kelly shook her head impatiently. "Not my implants. My goddess chest…"

"Good," Caddy said. "I never did like that thing. And just think, babes, it'll ruin her colour-scheme. She's got it all black and white. She's minimalist."

"It was the first thing we ever bought together. It was my *Valentine* present," Kelly wailed, refusing to be distracted by details of interior decoration.

"It was a horrible thing, babes," Caddy said firmly. "As soon as I saw it I knew you and Dave weren't going to last. If ever there was a bad omen, it was buying that chest. And what on earth it was painted with I don't know. It came off over everything. Ruined my pink Vivienne Westwood."

"It was covered in red ochre. It was ethnic," Kelly sniffed. "And," a faint flash of the old Kelly surfaced for a moment, "that was never a Vivienne Westwood. I don't care what they said on E-bay."

The goddess chest had once had pride of place in Kelly's bedroom. The walls were still painted a curious terracotta shade to tone with its background colour, the dull earthy red which, as Caddy had said, did indeed tend to come off on everything. On the front panel a rather clumsy hand had carved, in high relief, a female face, surrounded either by wild locks of hair, or, possibly, snakes. She was grinning and lolling her tongue in a way that suggested the last stages of strangulation, or, again possibly, dementia, and painted in horribly garish colours of gold and green. No one was quite sure why Kelly had been convinced that she was a goddess, and not even she had ever decided which goddess she was, but the box had been called the goddess chest from the first moment of its arrival in the house.

"Anyway," Kelly said, draining her glass, "I want her back."

"Now, babes…" Caddy began nervously.

"I don't care about the other stuff, I don't want anything *she's* touched, but I want my goddess back. And she wants to come back."

Caddy firmly put the cork back in the bottle of white wine, feeling her initial prescription might have been a mistake. Especially if Kelly had been seeking any other kind of chemical comfort before she got there. She was certainly in a funny mood. "I'll put the kettle on, shall I?" she trilled. "Nothing like a cuppa…"

"Are you still seeing that roadie?" Kelly asked. "The one with the van?"

"No," Caddy said without hesitation. And then, thinking quickly, she added, "He's gone abroad. Emigrated."

Fortunately Kelly was too wrapped up in her own troubles to inquire what country in the known world would have accepted him.

Caddy made a pot of green tea with the concentration she gave to every physical activity. She did not want to hear any more about Kelly's goddess. Kelly had been silly about that chest right from the start, attributing all kinds of opinions to it – according to Kelly the goddess liked yellow flowers, the brighter the better, and they had to be tied up with red wool. So there had always been at least one, and often several bunches of marigolds, or tulips in particularly crude shades of yellow in the bedroom, usually in various stages of decay, because Kelly never changed their water. She had also, to Caddy's certain knowledge, taken to leaving a saucer of milk and honey in front of the chest, and insisting that the goddess (or perhaps her snakes) drank it over night. Caddy would not have been surprised if one of Dave's reasons for moving out had been the constant fear of putting his foot into a sticky saucer in his own bedroom. It was the kind of thing that put a man off.

"You drink that up," she said, handing over the tea. "Now. Did you get your keys back from him?"

"Forgot to ask…" Kelly whimpered.

Caddy leaned over and snagged the Yellow Pages from the kitchen counter. She found "L" for "locksmith" and reached for the phone.

"But I've got his," Kelly said. She gave a weird little giggle.

Caddy's fingers froze on the first button. "What?"

"They were in his jacket," Kelly's voice no longer sounded plaintive. No longer – really – sounded like Kelly at all. "He took it off because he got quite hot moving all my furniture out. He just threw it down on the floor like he always does, did – and I hung it up for him, like I always do, did."

"And while you did that, you picked his pocket?" Caddy said, unbelievingly.

"He had my keys. I took his. Fair exchange." Kelly laughed. It was not her usual breathless giggle but a full-throated bay. It sounded like a much older woman's laugh. Possibly an older woman with serious mental problems. "So we could go round now and get my chest," she continued. "It's quite light, we can easily carry it outside between us, and get a taxi."

"A taxi driver's never going to have that in his cab, coming off all over his seats."

"Then we'll take it on the tube. Dave and I did that when we bought it. I can't manage it alone, or I'd have brought her home before."

"But Dave and *her* will be there."

Kelly shook her head. "No, they won't," she said positively.

Caddy took a mouthful of hot green tea. "No," she said firmly. There were limits to friendship, and breaking and entering definitely crossed them.

Kelly usually pleaded and pouted and whined when she wanted you to do something. She had never before, in Caddy's experience, picked up a large knife from the display on the kitchen wall and presented it point forwards to her friend, in a roughly jugular direction.

"Come on," she said.

And Caddy, her perfectly toned and admirably supple ankles trembling slightly, followed her friend out of the flat. The knife, by then, was tucked into Kelly's handbag, but Caddy wasn't going to risk anything.

She was hoping that she might see someone she could ask for help, but it was the middle of the afternoon. The streets were more or less empty (there were certainly no policemen visible) and the tube station was apparently unmanned. Kelly steered them carefully towards an empty carriage and no one, except an old lady who looked quite as mad as Kelly and would probably have joined the expedition, rather than going for help, if appealed to, got on.

By the time they reached their station, Caddy was resigned to going as far as Dave's flat. Somehow, once there, she was going to part Kelly from her handbag, and then run screaming…After all, Kelly would have to put the bag down when she picked up the chest.

Dave's new flat was in a pleasant, leafy – empty – street.

Both girls walked up the steps to the front door, and Kelly took the keys from her bag and unlocked it. The hallway was, as Caddy had said, all black and white. The walls and ceiling were white, a black lacquered table stood against the wall (piled with post, Caddy noticed, as if no one had had time to open it) and there were big black and white marble tiles on the floor. There was also, rather unexpectedly, a broad red trail running right across the middle of them.

"I said that chest would ruin her décor," said Caddy shakily. "They must have dragged it across the floor."

"That's not red ochre," said Kelly. She bent down and dabbled her fingers in it. Then she stood up and licked them deliberately, one by one. "It's not red ochre at all."

Caddy looked at her for a moment, watching her friend's mouth spread into a wide mirthless grin, while her tongue lolled out, impossibly long and red…

Then she turned and ran, screaming down the steps into the pleasant, leafy street, while behind her she heard Kelly – screaming too.

Or was she laughing?

Biographies

Our editor

Catherine Lenderi

Catherine Lenderi has been working as an English teacher since 1998 and has frequently been employed as a freelance editor / proofreader. She works with authors of various genres. In the "Books" section of her website, you can see some of the books she has recently worked on and the authors' testimonies regarding her services.
http://catsedits.weebly.com/

Our writers (in no particular order)

Charlotte Stirling – who doubles as our Cover Designer

Charlotte Stirling divides her time between Germany and Scotland with her husband, two children and a depressed Beagle. Her flash fiction has been published in Literary Orphans, Camroc Press Review and Spelk Fiction. When she isn't writing or baking cupcakes, she is thinking about writing, reading, designing book covers, gaming or watching dark, blood-splattered dramas like the Walking Dead, Ray Donavon and Sons of Anarchy.
http://tabby007.tumblr.com/
http://tabathadesign.tumblr.com/

S.A. Shields

S.A. Shields is a twenty something mother of three boys, who spends too much time writing and drinking coffee. Her debut novel, Don't Speak, is a mature young adult fiction, which tackles those dark teenage issues no one wants to speak about.
http://writersspill.weebly.com/

Chloe Hammond

Born in Liverpool in 1975, she grew up in West Wales. She studied Behavioural Sciences at the University of Glamorgan, but pestered her lecturers to allow her some modules of Creative Writing. Married, she now lives by the sea, just outside Cardiff, with two bonkers dogs and a suitably lazy cat. Diagnosed with anxiety and depression, she finally made time to write, finding writing a stimulation to help her through every crisis.
http://www.chloehammond-author.weebly.com/

W.D. Frank

From his humble beginnings in a Texas township, W.D. Frank has reached a level of literary genius that challenges God himself. Small town preachers quake in their boots when he approaches and children wet themselves in fear. The dread that he shall unleash upon you is but a tiny glimpse of his horrific literary power, muted only by his mercy, to protect your virgin eyes from permanent scarring.
http://frankthetank881.wix.com/wdfrank

Tina Rath

Tina lives in London with her husband and some cats. She has had around 60 short stories published, and has several novels, including a fantasy trilogy on the stocks. She has a PhD in *The Vampire in Popular Fiction,* she's an actress – recent jobs include Hideous Creature and Professional Yawner. Plus she's a story-teller as well as a writer and a Queen Victoria Lookalike.
http://www.christinarath.wordpress.com/

J. Cassidy

J. Cassidy used to be an oak tree growing in a park in England. She still likes to be decorated once a year. Pink, sparkly fluffles and rainbows make everything better.
https://6twistedbiscuits.wordpress.com/

Angelika Rust

Angelika Rust was born in Vienna in 1977. These days, she lives in Germany, with her husband, two children, a despotic couple of cats and a hyperactive dog. After having tried almost every possible job from pizza delivery girl to HR consultant, she now makes a living knowing a little English.
http://angelikarust.wordpress.com/

Adam Oster

Adam Oster writes tales of adventure where he can

pretend he's gone on wild excursions across time and space all for the purposes of coming up with an entertaining story. He also likes pizza.
http://www.fatmogul.com/

Bradley Darewood

Born just before Halloween, Bradley Darewood has a special love of the macabre. He writes everything from psychotic sorceresses to indigents in space. Oh, and W.D. Frank refers to him as man-candy. Keep an eye out for his upcoming fantasy novel.
http://www.nerdempire.org/

Cat Nicolaou

Cat Nicolaou lives with her family and many pets on a small island in Greece. She grew up surrounded by crystal clear blue waters and beautiful beaches. Living in such a peaceful area, she enjoys the idyllic setting around her. It is therefore not surprising that she likes to write romantic stories. Strolling by the seaside is where she gets all her inspiration. As an ever-romantic herself, she likes writing and reading stories with a happy ending, though she does torment her characters before they find a happy resolution.
http://catnicolaou14.wix.com/cat-nicolaou

Ken Alexopoulos

Ken eats food and hates being kicked in the crotch.

Jay Robbins

Jay Robbins was born in the 1980s. He is from Wyoming.

Yvonne Marjot

Yvonne Marjot was born in England, grew up in New Zealand, and now lives on a Scottish island. She has been making up stories and poems for as long as she can remember, and once won a case of port in a poetry competition (New Zealand Listener, May 1996). In 2012 she won the Britwriters Award for poetry, and her novels *The Calgary Chessman*, *The Book of Lismore* and *Walking on Wild Air* are published by Crooked Cat.
https://www.facebook.com/TheCalgaryChessman

A.E. Churchyard

Kira Morgana writes popular fantasy novels. Now she's branching out into Dark Urban/Paranormal Fantasy and Science Fiction with a touch of horror and this darker fiction can be found under A. E. Churchyard. Currently, she's working on various projects including Fantasy novels. All this AND she volunteers at a local Brownie Pack. Kira lives in South Wales, UK with her family and when she works out where her mind has gone, you will be the first to know!
https://tpsworld.wordpress.com/

T.M. Hogan

T.M. Hogan is a Greek Australian mum of three, who refuses to grow up. Grade-A crazy that makes life

explode with colour and noise. A blooming dark fantasy writer, Walking Through Darkness is her first story to be published, with a trilogy titled Ganymede in the works.
https://www.facebook.com/T-M-Hogan-490418697803077

Contents

Romantics Anonymous 1
    Bradley Darewood / Cat Nicolaou 1
    J Cassidy 29
El Hambre De Las Calaveras 31
    Charlotte Stirling 31
    S.A. Shields 37
Girl of my Dreams – A Saga of Failure 41
    Adam Oster 41
Rain 63
    Angelika Rust 63
i think i need a shower 65
    Bradley Darewood 65
Down The Drain 67
    Ken Alexopoulos 67
For the Love of Cats and Dogs 69
    S.A. Shields 69
Your World And Its Weather 87
    W.D. Frank 87
Buried Doll 89

Tina Rath	89
Johnny on the Spot	91
Yvonne Marjot	91
Number Six	95
Charlotte Stirling	95
Deleting Jessy	97
Angelika Rust	97
Burn	103
Ken Alexopoulos	103
Valentine's Day	105
T.M. Hogan	105
Sex in Santo Domingo	109
Bradley Darewood	109
Waiting	119
Chloe Hammond	119
Miss Angelika March	121
Charlotte Stirling	121
To Hell and Back	123
Jay Robbins	123
Eternal Love	139
Bradley Darewood	139

Miss Smith's Upgrade 141
    A. E. Churchyard 141

I Dream Of Rigor: A Heartwarming Tale Of Murder, Sex, And Snuggling 149
    W.D. Frank 149

Parsley, Sage, Rosemary and Skunk Cabbage 153
    Tina Rath 153

Man in a Can 155
    Chloe Hammond 155

Metamorphosis 163
    Angelika Rust 163

Agnés and Albertine 165
    Charlotte Stirling 165

The Number 173
    Bradley Darewood 173

The Chest 183
    Tina Rath 183

Biographies 189

Printed in Great Britain
by Amazon